Praise for **Brian Peters**

Latitude 47

"*Latitude 47* delivers all the grim violence and suspense expected in crime fiction – but it goes far beyond a simple whodunit by author Brian Peters' skillful weaving in of elements of history and metaphysics."

-IndieReader (4.5 out of 5 stars)

"A solid and compelling story that satisfies everything I want in a crime book. I was engaged and invested each step of the way and the further I read the quicker I wanted to read."

–Joseph Haeger, *Independent Book Review*

To Wander the Labyrinth

"This promising debut makes some bold moves, especially with the anti-heroic Clay, whose redemption is very much in doubt. A dark thriller that's more Kafkaesque claustrophobia than Hitchcockian suspense."

-Kirkus Review

"Extraordinary pacing pulls us into the story, while gritty realism keeps us there...an unforgettable saga with an unexpectedly satisfying (albeit dark) ending."

–Lawrence Kane, *ForeWord Magazine*

Latitude 47

Brian Peters

AASP Press, 2020
www.aasppress.com

Published by AASP Press

For more information:

www.aasppress.com

aasppress@gmail.com

Library of Congress Control Number: 2020910783

Library of Congress Cataloging-in-Publication Data

Peters, Brian, 1967 –

Latitude 47/

Brian Peters

p. cm.

Cover Design by Craig Maher

Manufactured in the United States of America

ISBN 978-0-9838572-2-8

1 2 3 4 5

For my family

Foul whisperings are abroad: unnatural deeds

Do breed unnatural troubles: infected minds

To their deaf pillows will discharge their secrets:

More needs she the divine than the physician.

God, God forgive us all!

-The Doctor, Macbeth, Scene 5, Act 1

Monday

Clay awoke to the unpleasant, metallic tang of blood in his mouth. He pushed himself into a sitting position. His lower lip was swollen – right there – he could feel it with his tongue, could taste the blood where the soft flesh had split. His hands checked for other cuts or bruises on his body. A hangover of sleeping pills and alcohol kept his thoughts stilted and sluggish. Memories, like memories from a dream, drifted through his head about where he might have gone and what he might have done during this latest sleepwalking excursion. There were vague recollections of rain, the sound and feel of an unending precipitation. But the rest of the memories remained vague. Not that he wanted to remember. It was better if he didn't. And he tried to focus his mind on other things, benign things, less upsetting images and memories.

The green glow of the alarm clock showed 4:03 a.m. Clay lay back down and rolled onto his side. The taste of blood worked like a magnet for a host of unwelcome images and sounds, recollections he wanted to dismiss as nothing more than lies of his imagination.

After a brief and frustrating attempt to sleep again, he turned and switched on the bedside lamp. His fingernails had dried dirt wedged under them. Digging.

Yes, he remembered now. The feel of the soil and how the rain had turned the black earth to mud; the sides of the hole sluffing down as he dug.

An angry cramp seized his calf and forced him to throw back the covers and grab the toes of his foot to stretch the muscle. The nighttime chill, along with walking outside in bare feet, often triggered this type of spasm. Clumps of dried mud littered the sheets near his feet.

"Goddamn it!" The words came out flat within the empty room.

His anger at himself felt a bit absurd; he could have rinsed off before getting into bed, though. The sandpaper-like texture of the soil mixed disagreeably with the softness of the cotton sheets. He made hard, angry sweeps at the dirt, but only managed to scatter the filth to other parts of the bedding. His sweatpants and gray University of Washington t-shirt sat in a clump near the bedroom door. He would have to throw those clothes away as he feared there might be more than mud on them.

Clay reached for a prescription bottle on the nightstand, inadvertently knocking it off and sending it rattling across the carpeted floor. Benzodiazepine. To calm his thoughts and maybe help him get back to sleep. One dose. He picked up the half-empty bottle, shook out an oval-shaped, baby blue pill and swallowed it with a bit of blood-tinged saliva.

In the renewed silence, the distant patter of rain wove its way into the windowless bedroom. Naked, he sat back in the bed, closed his eyes, and tried to focus on the steady rhythm of the rainfall. After a few calming moments, he reached over, turned the light off, and pulled the covers over himself, doing his best to ignore the speckled lumps of dried dirt scratching against his skin. How many sleepwalking episodes had he suffered through over the past couple of weeks? Four? Six? Not that it mattered. What was done was done. For now, he wanted to sleep.

To capture a little more rest before he headed into work. Rolling to his side, he watched the strange shadows cast by the green light of the clock: an alien terrain of shifting shapes and meaning.

When he was younger, the doctors had called these episodic events by various names: sleep arousal disorder, non-REM sleep parasomnia, somnambulism. Sleepwalking. These aberrant occurrences, according to the specialists, were supposed to end once he went through puberty. But when they didn't, the doctors performed an endless array of studies; one specialist tested him for epilepsy; another sent him to a sleep-disorder clinic where he slept in a sterile-white room wired to a polysomnography machine that measured his brain waves, eye movement, heart rhythm and muscle activity. One doctor, he clearly remembered, hadn't believed him at all, contending the night walking was a ploy for attention and not a physical ailment. The doctor recommended psychological testing and suggested counseling or some other form of psychotherapy.

And perhaps that last explanation hit closer to the truth than Clay wanted to admit. And so he forced these thoughts down, reminding himself, instead, about all those sleepwalking stories he had read over the years about the people who cooked four course meals while asleep, had sex with strangers, drove their cars into lakes and rivers, jumped from windows, got into fights, and, on rare occasions, committed violent crimes. The stories helped to reassure him of his sanity; he wasn't crazy; he was a sleepwalker; it didn't need to be any more complicated than that. Clay closed his eyes again and began to count backwards from a hundred.

Saturday

It felt like a waste of time, but Kiki scanned the names in the left-hand column of the accounting ledger anyway. The ledger dated from the mid-1800s and documented the debits and credits from one of Seattle's first brothels. In addition to mundane business expenses such as candle tallow and soap, the book contained the names of male patrons and the women they had paid to spend time with. The brothel's madame had written each entry in a looping, elegant cursive that gave the document an unjustified air of elegance.

The photocopied ledger had turned up in her grandmother's belongings, one piece of a much larger genealogy search that appeared to center on a man named Rueben. Her grandmother had highlighted the importance of the ledger in one of her notebooks. *Most of the men who came to Seattle during its early years,* her grandmother had written, *likely visited the brothel because of the lack of women in the area.* Kiki, vaguely, recalled her grandmother mentioning a distant family connection to one of Seattle's early settlers. But only vaguely. And despite the importance her grandmother had given the accounting document, Kiki had found no mention of anyone named Rueben.

She could have missed it, though. Her mind drifted so easily now. Nana's sudden death three weeks ago continued to have a heavy, unreal feel to it. Every time the phone rang, she expected to hear her voice on the other end. Her grandmother had raised her, given her a sense of family, a sense of having a place in the world. Where would she get that now? she wondered. She felt untethered. Lost. Kiki's mom had taken off not long after Kiki's birth. She had never met her father. And maybe that was part of the problem. Part of the reason she seemed unable to accept her grandmother's death as something natural.

A copy of the hospital's pathology report sat on the table next to her. It had arrived in the mail yesterday. The coroner listed the cause of death as a heart attack. Nana had been in her mid-sixties and overweight, and that made it convenient to pin her death on something as generic as a heart attack even though she had no history of heart disease, high blood pressure, or abnormally high cholesterol. In addition, no one seemed to care about the threatening phone calls she had complained of the week before she died. None of it, the police had told her, warranted an investigation. Kiki, however, refused to backdown. She had talked to a Seattle Police Department detective yesterday to go over several irregularities in the hospital's pathology report.

"I'm sorry for your loss," the detective had said before Kiki had time to explain herself, "I really am, but everything you're telling me is nothing more than coincidence. There is nothing-"

"Listen, please," Kiki had sensed the detective was about to hang up. "When I went to identify my grandmother's body, there were abrasions and bruising around her mouth, like something heavy had been pressed down on her face. And even the pathology report notes several broken fingernails and a significant bruise on her right arm."

"Yes, I know, you mentioned that already. But none of those things mean she was murdered. Your grandmother was old. Older people bruise very easily and there is no way to determine anything from a broken nail."

"But what about the bloodshot eyes? That is a textbook characteristic of suffocation. Am I right?"

"Hold on," the detective had said, the tone of his voice growing impatient, "I know you've lost someone. And I know how hard that is to deal with. I do. But there is nothing to investigate here. Period. You need to find a constructive way to deal with your grief and stop looking for some outside force to blame."

Kiki looked away from the ledger and stretched, unclenching her fists for the first time in an hour. She had known about Nana's interest in genealogy, but she never imagined the volume of photocopies, notebooks, and periodicals her grandmother had amassed. Stacks of this material now teetered on the verge of toppling off Kiki's clear-stained cedar table. She had collected every document and scrap of paper and brought it back to her apartment where it now spread across the glossy surface of the table like the alluvial plain of a great river on the verge of flooding everything around it.

Despite the lack of finding anything, the jumbled mass of material helped to occupy Kiki's thoughts. It gave her a reason to get up in the morning. Without it, she would still be in bed, lying there until she had to leave for work. That was how she had spent the first two weeks after her grandmother died.

Next to her on the table, a rough-hewn pine frame enclosed a faded, three-inch by five-inch Kodachrome print. The picture showed a four-year-old Kiki on her grandmother's lap looking at the camera and grinning; her grandmother's head tilts upwards, laughing at something inappropriate Kiki has said. She loved that picture. Each time she looked at it, she could hear her grandmother's rolling laughter. The photograph also reminded her how much she looked like her grandmother now. The soft, round facial features. The hazel, almond-shaped eyes. The earthen-brown coloring of her skin that confused people into assuming she was either Asian or Hispanic. She was neither. Her family descended from the Duwamish, the people who had once lived on the land that now made up the city of Seattle. Her grandmother had drilled this fact into Kiki's head from an early age: "Our people and this part of the world," her grandmother liked to lecture, "are as ancient and full of history as anywhere in China or Europe. This land is our home, stolen from under us by crooks and murderers."

Kiki stood up from the table and moved to the window. The misty rain mixed with the morning gray of the city, giving the outside world a grainy, blurred appearance. She rested her forehead against the cold glass and scanned the street below. Empty. Just a string of vacant cars parked along each side. That was good, though. Her shoulders relaxed a little as she still remembered the man in the hooded sweatshirt standing across the street earlier that morning. She had spotted him not long after getting home from an exhausting ten-hour swing shift at the hospital. At one in the morning, the sight of the figure triggered her anxiety, making her wonder if he had been waiting there for her. The muted streetlights had made it impossible to see anything but a vague outline of a face beneath the hood. And when the man tilted his head back and appeared to look in the direction of her apartment, she found herself stumbling away from the window and scrambling to lock the door and turn off the lights. After giving herself a moment to calm down, and keeping within the shadows of the living room, she had returned to the window only to find the stranger gone.

Even now, she questioned what she had seen. It had been late; she had been tired. Part of her wondered if the figure had been waiting there for her? Another part of her wondered if she had imagined the whole thing, mistaking the movements of the trees and the wind and the rain for those of a real person? Maybe the police were right, perhaps her grief had clouded her reasoning.

Monday

Clay entered the newsroom through the stairwell door. The open floor plan of the space spread out in front of him like the honeycomb of a hive. Pods of desks clustered together to form the different sections of the paper – sports, metro, arts, business – each individual desk separated by a set of four-foot high partitions. The cylindrical cement supports created the only visual break from the sea of desks; the offices along the windowed perimeter blocked most of the exterior light.

Clay glanced at the wall clock above the exit: 9:40. He was late. Melissa, the metro editor, would notice and likely say something to him. Not that he cared. Her rote reprimands represented nothing more than mild annoyances. And if it weren't a Monday, she would probably let it go. But since he was the lead crime reporter, Mondays meant checking to make sure nothing had been overlooked by the weekend staff. He should have been here at eight thirty to call his police contacts, and then let Melissa know if anything had been missed before she went to the morning news meeting at 9:00. That wasn't going to happen today.

From where he stood, he could see Melissa's desk. It was empty. She was probably still at the meeting. If the meeting went long, he might have enough time to call his contacts and type up a budget if the weekend reporters had missed anything critical. He might still get out of this without much of a hassle.

The clatter of typing and half-muffled voices vibrated through the open space as he walked to his desk. About three-quarters of the reporters were in the newsroom. The rest were likely out working on a story or would be coming in later to cover meetings.

At his desk, he shook off the excess rain from his jacket and draped it over the back of the chair. The late dose of medication continued to keep his thoughts slow and chalky despite several cups of strong coffee. He hoped work would help divert his thoughts from the previous night's memories. The reflective black screen of the computer monitor created a fisheye-lens effect on his face and the surrounding newsroom. He hadn't had time to take a shower. He made a half-hearted attempt to fix his hair but quickly gave up and pushed the computer's power button. The whir of the machine's fan joined with the rest of the newsroom's ambient white noise.

"How was your weekend, Clay?" The unexpected sound of Melissa's high-pitched voice startled him.

He swiveled the chair around. She stood there with her arms crossed and a scowl on her face. "Fantastic," he answered with feigned enthusiasm. "And you?"

"Crap. Too much Chianti." Her red curly hair had a slightly bewitched appearance. And because of her short stature, he was nearly eye to eye with her while still sitting in the chair. "By the way, thank you for being so punctual this morning. I'm assuming you did the follow-up calls from your apartment since I didn't see you here earlier."

"Sorry, I'm getting to those now. I just got back from an interview that went longer than I'd planned," he lied.

"Sure," she said, her expression darkening. "Which story was that for?"

"The crime statistics story."

"Good. Then I can expect you to finish that by the end of the week? I could use it for Friday's paper."

"No, I've got a lot more reporting to do. I thought we talked about running the story on the last Sunday of this month?"

A pained smile creased Melissa's face. "What if we shortened the story to twenty-five inches? Could you manage that by Thursday?"

"Maybe. But I've got the ride-alongs with Detective Carpenter set for this week and next. I'm going to need that to put a face to the statistics. Like we'd talked about."

"Right." She leaned against his desk. Her mood seemed worse than normal. "Then what do you have for me this week? Anything?"

He paused a moment to make sure his response didn't sound disrespectful. "I'm going by police headquarters in the next hour. I'll see if I can dig something up."

His response only seemed to harden her aggravation. "Find me a story, Clay," she said. "Demonstrate to me that someone in this goddamn newsroom is at least trying to be productive —"

"Let me make a few calls," he interrupted. "I'll come up with something." Clay picked up the phone and dialed the downtown precinct number. If he had hoped this would get her to leave, it didn't happen. She remained standing there, apparently waiting for him to talk to someone. It wasn't until he got ahold of the swing-shift sergeant and began to ask questions about the weekend that she finally headed over to her desk.

By the time he finished making a handful of calls, he had a lead on a string of assaults in Ballard that had gone unreported. Clay typed a budget line for the attacks and added a note that he would update it when he returned from the precinct office. For now, he needed to leave to avoid showing up late to his meeting with Detective Carpenter. It had come as something of a surprise when the detective agreed to let Clay shadow him on a homicide investigation. Several other detectives had refused.

Detective Carpenter had been an option of last resort. Clay had expected the detective to turn him down, particularly since the detective had never shown much patience for him. He didn't understand the detective motives, but he also didn't want to make the man wait and give him an excuse to pull out of the arrangement.

The pale fluorescent light of the newspaper building gave way to the overcast of the morning sky as Clay walked to the employee parking lot. The rain had stopped. The world showed gray in all directions. No sign of the Olympic Mountains in the west or the Cascades in the east. He should hate it: the overcast. So many people did. The colorless winter landscape that loomed over Seattle in a nearly uninterrupted stretch starting in September and going on through to the end of May. He liked the gray. The infinitely subtle variations of gray that felt like an extension of his own murky thoughts.

The air had a pleasantly cool feel. The growl of traffic and the cries of seagulls swirled with the smell of saltwater, tar, and the diesel exhaust of the nearby ferries. Inside his car, he started the old Volkswagen motor, the loud rattle of the engine obliterating all other sounds.

The drive to the Seattle Police Department's headquarters had an interminable feel to it as Clay slowed and stopped at a fourth consecutive traffic light. A trip of some three dozen blocks looked like it might take twenty minutes. Despite leaving plenty of time, he may still end up late. That should have generated some anxiety; but it barely registered. His thoughts, instead, focused on the vague memories of his early-morning wandering. Not just the digging. But the swollen lip. The taste of blood.

Idling there at the light, Clay's eyes locked onto a dead seagull near the center of the intersection. The bird had a single wing cocked at a forty-five-degree angle and appeared almost alive as its feathers waved in the rush of air caused by the passing cars and trucks. But the illusion of life ended at the bird's crushed torso and the unblinking black eyes. Raising a hand from the steering wheel, Clay gestured in the direction of the bird as if to urge it out of the middle of traffic. That was all it needed, he thought. A little encouragement.

The traffic light changed, but Clay struggled to come back to the present, to get past the noise of words in his head, his eyes still focused on the bird, part of him hoping to see the bird stand and take flight again.

The nondescript stone edifice of the Seattle Police Department headquarters blended seamlessly into the surrounding gray, making it almost invisible. Clay checked in at the front desk and took a seat in the small waiting area. He had arrived with a couple of minutes to spare. Not that it had mattered. Detective Carpenter, according to the desk sergeant, was in a meeting and wouldn't be available for another fifteen minutes.

Clay began to look through his notebook at the interviews he had already completed for the crime statistics story. These included a brief Q and A with the chief of police and interviews with two community organizers. None of these, however, offered anything of much interest, other than the typical complaints: the police chief advocated for more officers and a bigger budget for the department's gang unit; the community activists wanted more funding for intervention and after-school programs. He could have come up with these responses even without the interviews.

When he first pitched the story to Melissa about the escalation of violent crime in the city's Central District neighborhood, it had drawn little more than an indifferent shrug. "No one wants to read a stat-burdened article about crime in the poorer areas of the city," she said. "Those aren't our readers."

Her reaction wasn't a surprise. She just didn't understand. The people or place of the violence had little to do with it, as far as Clay was concerned. That aspect of the story was irrelevant. The violence itself interested him; the people experiencing the violence; those committing the violent acts; the growth and expansion of the violence.

So Clay narrowed the focus of the story to an eight-block section where violent crime – homicide, rape, assault – had tripled over a five-year period. The area also sat at the fringes of the city's rapid gentrification. And this, he had explained to Melissa, mattered a great deal to the newspaper's readers because the violence was happening not far from their backdoors.

"It might work," she had said, "but you're still left with a dry, limp story about numbers."

"I've talked to one of the homicide detectives and he's agreed to let me shadow him on a murder investigation from that area. I'll be able to tell the story through the eyes of the victim as well as those who live in that area."

"Better reporters than you have tried and failed at these types of projects," she had warned him. "I don't want you to spend a bunch of time on this and then have nothing worthwhile to show for it. You understand me?"

Detective Carpenter was the lead on most of the homicides in the Central District, and, after twenty years in the Seattle Police Department, he knew these streets as well as anyone. In that respect, he was a good fit for the story. But Clay's interactions with the detective had never seemed to go well, leaving it unclear whether the detective's brusque manner was directed at Clay personally or at people in general.

When the desk sergeant finally gave him permission to go up, it was an hour past the scheduled appointment time.

With a soft knock on the open door, Clay took a step into the detective's office. The detective was studying the contents of a folder spread out on his desk, which, like the rest of the space, had a tight, orderly appearance.

"What kind of sensational bullshit are we feeding the masses today?" the detective asked as he looked up.

"I thought we were meeting at 10:30?" The words came out clipped. Clay knew he needed to play nice with the detective, but the annoyance of wasting an entire hour made it difficult to conceal his frustration.

"Busy! I believe you're aware of the increase in violent crimes over the past couple of years. And if this time doesn't work for you, I'm happy to reschedule our meeting for 11:30 tomorrow. Does that work better?"

"No, this works fine, it's just—"

"Stop. No justs. This either works or it doesn't."

Clay took a breath and attempted to calm himself. "It works."

Even after two years of off-and-on interaction, Clay felt uneasy around the detective. The man was in his mid-forties and had a broad face and a flat nose that looked like it had been broken more than once. He stood 6' 2" tall and weighed north of 200 pounds. Clay knew the detective had fought in Vietnam and that the man was divorced and had two teenage girls going to school on the Eastside. But it was more than the man's size and vague history that bothered Clay. There was an air of distrust about him. In past encounters, the detective had made comments and thrown looks in Clay's direction that made it seem as though he suspected Clay of something criminal. He felt a bit of that now, in fact. And he tried to push past the feeling, dismissing it as another symptom of his dysfunctional morning.

"For the ride-along, I thought we might focus on the double homicide from last Thursday," Clay suggested. "Or did you have something else in mind?" He remained near the doorway waiting for the detective to invite him in. He had already started things off poorly and didn't want to make any additional mistakes.

"Actually," the detective said and glanced back at the folder on his desk, "I thought I'd drop you off somewhere in the middle of the CD and let you wander around for a while. Maybe you could become your own crime victim and write a first-person account of your experience." The detective smiled. "How's that sound?"

"That would make a great follow-up piece." And Clay tried to give a smile of his own, though it felt more like a grimace. "For this story, though, I need someone else's crime scene. You did say you would help me. Are you still okay with that?"

The detective leaned back in his chair and gave Clay a hard glare. "Remind me again of what I agreed to?"

"I'm going to shadow you on one of your homicide investigations, one that centers on that eight-block area in the Central District I mapped out for you."

"Right," the detective said. "I guess I recall something like that."

"Are we okay with the double homicide?"

"The two brothers."

"Yes."

"I forget, did your paper publish anything on the deaths of those two young black men?"

"I wrote something on it."

The detective fanned out a group of photographs from the folder and turned them so Clay could see the images right side up. Crime scene photos. Blood. A lot of blood sprayed across a carpeted floor. Two bodies. A thin, young black man in one picture. Another young black man in the other. A third photograph showed the two bodies crumpled up on the floor next to each other. "I must have missed that article. Was it on the front page? I don't read the front page."

"It was a brief at the back of the metro section."

"A brief. That's it? Two people murdered in their own home and that's all they get!"

"It wasn't my — "

16

"I knew those boys. Were you aware of that?"

"No. I'm sorry," he said, the words coming out with an air of distraction.

"Good kids. That's them in the photographs."

Clay stared at the pictures with a growing sense of unease. Not because of the blood. Not because of the obtuse angle of the bodies, or the massive head trauma, or the open eyes. It came from something else, perhaps the twitch of excitement he experienced looking at the photographs, or, maybe, the vague familiarity of the scene.

"You're right about that little area being a pocket of violence," the detective said, scooping up the photos with his large, black hands and returning them to the folder. "By the way, I've been reminded by command that you are not to quote me without a prior okay or print anything that might jeopardize the homicide investigation. Got that? Any quotes about this case or anything else police-related have to go through me and the communication department for approval."

"Okay."

"I'm not finished," the detective said, meeting Clay's gaze. "Remember the story about the body found in Discovery Park? You did everything but put my name on it when you included the details about the bite marks and the signs of sexual assault. If you ever do some generic attribution bullshit that everyone knows is me again, not only do we end our lovely relationship here, but I make sure you get a traffic ticket every day for the next year. Is there any confusion on this?"

"No. But I talked—"

"I don't want excuses," the detective snapped. "I want our roles clearly understood. I'm the one who stands to lose by bringing you into this homicide case. And since I knew these boys, this investigation is particularly important to me. Are we clear?"

Clay paused a moment and fought the urge to argue back. As much as the detective's condescending tone angered him, he didn't want to jeopardize the story over some avoidable power trip. "Yes, we're clear."

The detective hesitated for a moment as if debating whether to extend the lecture.

"I know you don't have to do this," Clay added. "And the last thing I want to do — "

"I'll be honest," the detective interrupted, "I don't have a lot of patience for your paper. And that includes its reporters. There's just something about you people that doesn't sit right with me. Maybe it's all the questions and poking around that makes me uneasy. I don't know. Anyway, I'm doing this because the story needs to be told. People need to understand what's happening in these neighborhoods and how this violence impacts human beings and not just a bunch of dismissible numbers. So don't fuck this up. Clear?"

"I understand."

"If you haven't done so already, make sure to look at the police department's overtime budget from the past five years. As crime has gone up, the city has cut overtime. Have you looked at those numbers?"

"Not recently."

"It's a good thing I made copies, then." The detective picked up a stapled set of papers and tossed them to Clay. "The last thing I want to see in that story of yours is some suggestion that this is a failure of the police department."

"Okay. Is that it?" Clay asked. He tried to keep the impatience from his voice.

The detective closed the folder on his desk and stood up. "That's it for now. I hope you have a strong stomach. The house is a bloody mess. You can still feel the violence hanging over that place."

Monday Afternoon

Kiki took a bite of toast and followed that with a sip of honey-sweetened black tea. The nightshift at the hospital didn't start for another two hours. An eternity, she thought. She preferred being at work. The routine made it easier to push aside unpleasant thoughts. Since her grandmother's death, she had picked up as many extra shifts as she could. Today, however, there was only her set schedule.

The brothel ledger sat off to the side; its list of names, as it had on the previous day, blurred from one set of looping black lines to another. She struggled to understand what she expected to find in that mess of information. Her grandmother's killer? Some vague connection to the past? Or, like the police detective had suspected, was she looking for an excuse to not deal with her grandmother's absence? Kiki had to remind herself, again, of the threatening phone calls Nana had received prior to her death, and her grandmother's suspicion the calls had something to do with her research into the family's past.

Taking another sip of tea, Kiki pulled the accounting book back in front of her. A whorehouse, even at the very edge of the world, was a busy place. As she scanned the page, an idea struck her that maybe she was hunting the wrong ghosts. Instead of stalking the dead, maybe she should look for someone who might still be alive. Like her mother. The last time she saw her was more than seventeen years ago when she showed up looking lost and desperate. Kiki had been thirteen at the time and her mother had brought a shabby-looking teddy bear as a gift. The real reason for the visit, Kiki found out later, was to ask Nana for money. That was the last she had heard from her mother. She hadn't shown up for Nana's funeral. No flowers. No note or card.

As for her father, Kiki had heard rumors over the years about him living somewhere in the Dakotas laboring in the oil fields or working as a wrangler on a ranch in Montana.

These thoughts rose and fell, growing tangled and confused with the numerous names listed in the ledger. Kiki's eyes wandered to the right-hand column of the page where salacious notes chronicled a customer's experience, including the name of the female companion, the length of time spent with that woman, and the amount of money paid for the visit. Some of the more frequent patrons had additional notes written in the margins such as alcohol preferences, favorite perfume scent, or any unusual fetishes. Within these notes, the sterile, inventory-like layout of the ledger became unpleasantly alive. On a typical Friday or Saturday night, most of the women saw a man just about every hour starting as early as one in the afternoon and going on as late as three in the morning. The rhythmical wheeze of the bedsprings along with the knocking headboards must have filled the building like an angry haunting. By the time the last man left, Kiki imagined, the once-white bed sheets must have turned an oily yellow. The smell of soap replaced with the toxic odor of sweat and male ejaculate. Kiki wondered if the women felt relief when a man finished or dread at the knowledge that another was already creeping up the stairs to insert himself inside of her.

In a nearby notebook, Kiki absently scribbled the lines of a biblical quote her grandmother liked to use whenever Kiki had done something wrong or was being stubborn:

If I wash myself with snow,
And cleanse my hands with lye,
Yet you will plunge me in the ditch.

After a half-attentive scan, she flipped to the next page, indifferent about whether she had finished the previous page or not. Then she spotted it. Third name from the top. A tingle of surprise rippled across the surface of her skin. Right there. Under the column that listed the names of the prostitutes. Each letter written like all the others in the same colorless swirling cursive loops. But this was a name Kiki recognized. She leaned forward to make sure she hadn't misread it. There it was, though, a woman with the same Duwamish name as her mother, Lalaida. A hundred years before her mother was born, someone else had carried the burden of that unlucky name. It made Kiki's hands shake. Like seeing an apparition. Her mother's name, Kiki recalled her grandmother saying, had come from a great-great-grandmother. Nana, however, had never mentioned anything about a brothel. Kiki picked up her pen and wrote down the date and time of the name's appearance, her handwriting almost unreadable from the shock of surprise. At the ledger, she traced her finger to the client's name: it started with what looked like an R, but the rest of the name was illegible. She returned to the list of prostitutes. There were two other entries for Lalaida that night. A quick scan of the previous three pages produced no other listings. Flipping forward, she found the name again a week later. There were five entries on that day, a Friday. And as if she wasn't agitated enough, the fourth entry clearly listed the customer's name as Reuben. Like the sandwich. Like the name Nana had been looking for. Kiki wrote down each of the four entries, including the

21

customer names and any other listed details. Over the next couple of months of ledger entries, the name Lalaida appeared two dozen more times. This included several additional pairings with a client named Rueben.

The last appearance was on Monday, February 15. There were four entries for Lalaida that day. And the customer's name on the final entry was Reuben. Kiki scribbled a note to look at the newspapers around that date. And that was it. Despite checking three different times, there were no other entries for a woman named Lalaida, or a man named Rueben. There were no notes next to the man's name, either, which suggested he hadn't patronized the brothel all that often.

Had they gone off together? Or was this nothing more than a coincidence?

Within the agitated search for the names, Kiki had lost track of time. When she lifted her head from the mess spread out in front of her, she had less than fifteen minutes to get ready for work.

A sound close to laughter escaped Kiki's lips as she stood up from the table. It felt unreal. Like a hallucination. She leaned over and looked at the ledger again. Lalaida was still there. And there was Reuben. It seemed absurd to consider these two names somehow connected to her and her family. She turned and headed to the bathroom to take a quick shower. And what if they were connected? What did it prove? Did it even matter? From the corner of her eye, Kiki saw the golden winter glow of the sun coming through the windows. No rain. Not yet.

Monday

The black, unmarked sedan turned right off East Madison Street and onto Martin Luther King Jr. Way. A dull silvery gray spread across the early-afternoon sky. The detective took another right a few minutes later and traveled several more blocks before parking in front of a dilapidated, mid-century bungalow. Flaccid yellow police tape encircled the narrow front entry.

"Don't touch anything. Don't step on anything. Don't lean over and breathe on anything," the detective lectured. "Clear? Forensic has been through the place but no one has given the go-ahead for cleanup."

Clay nodded. The surrounding neighborhood, somewhat to his surprise, wasn't the rundown mess he expected. The houses were modest in size and looked to have been built in the thirties and forties. A fair number of the yards and homes had a neat, well-maintained appearance. Most. Not all. For every four well-cared-for homes there was a residence with a collapsing porch, gang graffiti across the front façade, and a collection of bottles and cans and paper tangled within a thick web of uncontrolled shrubs and weeds, as if nature itself wanted to swallow the blighted structure whole.

"You don't have a weak stomach, do you?"

"No." Clay stepped out of the car. The air smelled of rain.

A group of kids played football on a small strip of grass in a nearby yard. The game, however, slowed to a stop as all eyes focused on Clay and the detective. The detective held up a hand in the direction of the kids and waved. Several in the group offered a tentative wave back, which seemed enough of a signal to resume play. Gradually, the sound of adolescent voices filled the air again, softening the edges of the colorless landscape.

The detective started across the street. "If you get sick in there, I will personally make sure forensics takes a sample of it and adds you to the list of suspects."

"I'll be fine." The words came out perhaps a little too confident. He worried about the smells within the home, particularly the smell of blood and human waste.

The house, with its white paint and light-blue trim, needed work. The white paint had chipped off in places, particularly near the ground where carpet-like cap moss grew on the exposed and rotting wood. The wooden steps to the front door sagged. An overgrown hedge filled up the right side of the yard, blocking half of the house from view. There wasn't much of a front yard. Weeds mostly. Clay took out his notebook and jotted down a couple of lines of description. Being here with the detective, having the opportunity to get so close to the crime scene, had generated the strangest mix of excitement and anxiety. A nervous cramp twisted his stomach. His palms were moist. From the photos, he knew there would be a lot of blood since the killer had shot both men in the head at point-blank range. The smells. He prepared himself for the metallic, musty odor of death.

The detective walked past the front porch and continued along the side of the house towards the backyard where a chain-link gate stood open. An acrid stench emanated from the back of the house and forced Clay to cover his mouth and nose with the sleeve of his coat. At the gate, the long, narrow yard was nothing more than a muddy stretch of torn-up earth and dog excrement.

24

Two doghouses and a rusty 50-gallon oil drum sat at the back of the space.

"What happened to the dogs?" Clay asked.

The detective pointed to spots of blood-red dirt. "Dead. Both dogs were shot the night of the murders."

"Did the police do that?"

"No, it was the shooter. The dogs were dead when I got here."

"Were you the first one to arrive?"

"Just about."

Mud and rain had buckled the bottom of the wood-veneer backdoor, part of the veneer starting to peel away. The detective shoved the door open and crouched underneath the yellow crime-scene tape. Clay hesitated. He brought his arm away from his mouth and nose and could taste the smell of decaying animal waste. A touch of lightheadedness hit him as he ducked under the tape and entered a small kitchen area. In his notebook, he scribbled a reminder to get a photographer out here. This house, this murder scene, would serve as the framework for the crime-statistics story. He already felt certain of that.

Inside, the odors shifted to stale alcohol and cigarette smoke. Beer cans, playing cards, and one- and five-dollar bills littered the yellow and white linoleum floor. An upended ashtray had left cigarette butts and ash covering the circular kitchen table. This was where the violence had started, he thought. Three metal-framed kitchen chairs were overturned and scattered to different points in the room. Several cupboard doors were open. Dirty dishes spilled from the metal sink.

Detective Carpenter continued through the kitchen and into the adjacent living room. Two asymmetrically shaped bloodstains colored a broad swath of the tan carpet. A metallic tang hung in the air. The smell of human incontinence. So much blood. Clay's stomach tightened. On the wall adjacent to the carpet stains, blood arced across the white surface like a macabre rainbow. He stepped back, but not because the sight upset him. Instead, he tried to take it all in. It was true about the sensation of violence still looming in the house. It seemed to vibrate through the space.

Clay avoided the spots of blood and went over next to the detective, who stood at a street-facing window, his eyes focused on something outside.

A smile spread across the detective's face when he turned and looked at Clay. "You need a moment? Hard as it is to believe but you look paler than normal," the detective laughed. "I'm warning you, go outside if you're going to get sick."

"I'm not going to get sick," Clay said, attempting to push past his agitated excitement. "The press release on this called it a gang shooting. Is that still the assumption?"

"In this neighborhood, if we're not sure what happened, it's always going down as gang related."

"Any suspects?"

"Suspects! How long have you been doing this job?"

"Long enough. Why?"

"How many gang-related homicides have we solved four days after the shooting?"

Clay shrugged, his eyes drawn back to the area of blood. It surprised him how the sight of blood barely elicited a reaction. The smells did, but not the blood.

"In neighborhoods like this, fear is the guiding factor, not justice. If anyone saw anything, they aren't talking about it to the police."

"Is this a typical crime scene for a gang shooting?"

"It's typical from the standpoint a gun was fired, and young black men were killed."

"It looks more like an execution. Not a drive-by."

"An execution? What makes you say that?"

Clay hesitated, catching a mocking tone in the detective's voice. "The blood spots on the carpet are side by side. The brothers must have been next to each other and shot about the same time. And by the low blood

26

splatter on the wall the victims were probably kneeling when they were killed."

"All right. That's a decent guess. What else, Kojak?"

"The front door."

"What about it?"

"It's intact. No sign of forced entry. I'm guessing the shooter was a part of the group playing cards in the kitchen, so the brothers must have known him."

The detective chuckled and motioned for Clay to follow him back into the kitchen. "Good theories. You're missing a couple of important details. For one, the shooter wasn't sitting at the table with the victims. And while the shooter might have known the brothers, I don't think they knew him."

"Why do you say that?"

"Do you like puzzles?" the detective asked, pushing at one of the fallen kitchen chairs with his foot.

"I suppose."

"I love a good puzzle, especially those thousand-piece puzzles where a dark night sky takes up half of the picture. You ever try to do one of those?"

Clay shook his head no.

"The start of a criminal investigation is a lot like the moment you dump the entire puzzle out on the table. Everything is jumbled up, the important pieces indistinguishable from the unimportant," the detective said, going over and looking at the sink full of dishes. "Do you understand what I'm saying?"

"Not really."

"How many chairs do you see?"

"Four."

"And how many of those chairs are knocked over?"

"Three."

"But we only have two victims, right? That means there were at least four people in this house at the time of the killing. And forget about the condition of the front door because the shooter entered through the back."

"If that's true, why doesn't the door show any damage, then?"

"The lock on the door is broken. The killer only had to turn the knob to enter the house. Now look at the chairs. These boys were trying to get out of the kitchen and to the front door. And don't forget about the dogs. The shooter killed the dogs prior to entering the house."

"Okay. But how do you get four? The shooter could have been at the table with the brothers and gotten upset at something while they were playing cards. Maybe he shot the dogs after the killings."

"The couch," the detective said.

"The couch?"

The detective returned to the living room. An overstuffed navy-blue couch sat in the middle of the room facing a shabby entertainment center. Stains covered much of the couch's fabric surface; wads of white filling spilled out of three of the four back cushions.

"You see the round indentation marks in the carpet? Those are two feet from where the couch is now. And look at how clean the carpet is between those indentations and where the couch sits. That couch hadn't been moved in a very long time."

Clay nodded.

"The shooter, I'm guessing, pushed one of the three men onto the couch. And that guy must have weighed well over two-fifty given how far the couch moved. Even if both of those skinny brothers were thrown against the couch at the same time, it never would have moved that far."

"Could there have been two shooters?"

The detective frowned. "Do you want to hear this or not?"

"Sorry."

The detective pointed at several bullet holes in the frame of the front door. "It looks like the killer shot at the three men to stop them from getting out the door. He then brought them back to this area, pushed the big dude onto the couch, and then forced the two brothers to kneel." The detective gestured to a couple of small bloodstains not far from the larger set of splatter marks. "It also appears as if the killer shot one of the boys in the leg. That would account for these other bloodstains."

"Why?"

"Who knows? He might have shot him as the three rushed the door. Or maybe the brothers weren't cooperating. It's also possible the shooter just enjoyed inflicting pain. But not long after that, with the brothers still kneeling, the shooter executed them with shots to the head."

The blood looked almost wet. Clay fought the urge to reach down and touch it. "So why aren't there three bodies? Why let the guy on the couch live?" he asked. A complex mixture of filth and oxidized iron tainted the air.

"My guess is the shooter used the third man to pass along a message to someone, possibly a dealer the two boys were connected with."

Clay glanced out the living room window to the cloudy winter day. "So how are you going to track down this third guy?"

"Finding him won't be the problem. The hard part will be getting him to talk." The detective knelt and picked at something on the carpet. "You were right about one thing; this wasn't a random drive-by. The shooter knew what he was doing." The detective studied whatever it was he had taken from the carpet. "He used a silencer. That's how he shot the dogs in the backyard without alerting the three inside. And he also had plastic bags over his shoes."

"Bags?"

The detective stood up. "Look over here." He pointed at a smudge of blood on the carpet. "He walked through the blood on his way out the front door, but there aren't any tread marks. He came to this house knowing he was going to kill these boys."

The detective went on to give several more examples of how the shooter had avoided leaving any evidence behind. Then he said something that brought Clay back into the conversation. He said the word "California."

"Like some sort of an interstate gang war?" he asked. He could already hear Melissa's whoop of enthusiasm at the story possibilities this presented.

"Settle down. It's purely hypothetical at this point. We get California gangbangers coming up this way all the time looking to carve out their own territory. In the end, this might be nothing more than a low-level drug hit. It just doesn't have that feel to it, though. I've never seen a gang shooting quite this methodical. You all right?"

"What?"

The detective pointed down at Clay's hand. "You're bleeding."

He had scratched open a scab on the back of his hand. Blood had welled up and started to drip down his skin. He rubbed the blood away and then wiped both hands against his pants. He checked the carpet around him to make sure nothing had reached the floor. "Nerves, I guess." But it wasn't nerves. It was more about the rush of violence that still filled the space. The intoxication of it.

"You need to step outside?"

"I'm fine," he said.

"You don't look fine."

"It's okay. I've seen this sort of thing before."

"Really?" There was a note of surprise in the detective's voice. "What other cop has let you view a fresh crime scene?"

Outside the window, the wind blew a scattering of brown leaves across the front yard. "The first newspaper job I had out of school was covering crime in north-central Idaho. I was able to document a couple of homicides prior to the bodies even being removed."

The detective asked another question, but Clay didn't want to say anything more about what he had seen or what had happened. He took out his notebook and scribbled down details about the interior of the house, the location of the bloodstains, the knocked-over chairs. "What was it like when you got here? Was there a lot of commotion? Were there any people in the streets?"

"There were a few neighbors looking on."

"But no witnesses?"

"No, no witnesses."

Clay asked a couple of more questions about the neighborhood and received a series of vague answers from the detective.

"You said you knew the brothers?"

"A little. They were always together. If you saw one, the other was somewhere nearby," the detective answered. His normally commanding voice dropped slightly as he talked. "Small-time dope dealers. That was all. Nothing violent. They actually came across as well behaved. Even a little bit awkward. Not your hard-nosed gangster. Nothing like that."

"Did they grow up around here?"

"From what I know, they pretty much raised each other. Dad in jail. Mom not all that involved. Both had done short stints in juvy and downtown." The detective took a deep breath. "I'll be honest, I got a little upset when I arrived on the scene and realized who had been killed."

"Why is that?"

"Are you not listening!" the detective snapped. "These were decent boys who got killed for no good reason. By the way, if you want to know more about who these young men were, you should talk with some of the neighbors. In the meantime, I've got more pressing issues today than babysitting you. We're done here."

Clay took a step back to give the detective room as he stalked towards the kitchen and out the backdoor. After taking one last slow look around, Clay put his notebook away and followed the detective. He could fill in the crime scene details when he got back to the newsroom. There was very little of this he was going to forget.

On the walk to the car, it took a moment for Clay to reorient himself to the outside world. It was difficult to gauge how long he had been in the house. It didn't feel long. Less than fifteen minutes, maybe. But the air outside felt colder and the gray of the overcast had darkened. The boys who had been playing football were gone as well. But other parts of his surroundings felt different, too. Sounds were sharper. Smells had a stronger edge, making the ambient air tarter, almost sour. The violence within the house had quickened his thoughts with a twisted kind of rush that felt uncomfortably familiar. He considered going home for more medication to blunt the agitation, to calm his thoughts.

Detective Carpenter stopped next to the car and looked down the street, perhaps searching for the boys from earlier. The kids were probably hiding, waiting until the strangers left since they should have all been in school at that time of day.

"Sorry if it felt like I was grilling you back there," Clay said, coming up next to the detective. "Reporter's habit. It's sometimes hard to know when to stop asking questions."

"That's all right. I don't usually let this type of thing get under my skin like that."

"Is there ever an easy homicide?"

"Most crime scenes are just another day at the office. I've seen enough blood and death to not get too caught up in the emotions of it. In this case, though, those boys deserved better."

Clay nodded and wondered at the quiet of the surrounding neighborhood. The silence had a jarring effect after the sight of so much violence.

"You did all right in there," the detective said. "I'll give you that. You ready for the next step?"

"What's that?"

"I'm doing recon this Friday to hunt down associates of the two brothers. You'll want to see this world at night, anyway. Everything changes when the dark comes. And remember, I'm trusting you on this," the detective said, turning his attention to Clay. "People need to know what's going on in these neighborhoods, and I'm expecting you to do this story right. Understood?"

"I'll do my best."

"And bring your big-boy pants. You never can tell what's going to happen on a Friday night."

Wednesday

The long rectangular windows of the downtown library offered a view of the winter rain as it bled the city of color and depth. Kiki glimpsed a man and a woman walking by along Madison Avenue, the woman holding an umbrella that only kept their inside shoulders dry.

A muffled cough issued from one of the two other people in the library's musty-smelling Special Collections' room.

Kiki looked at the notepad to her left and saw the words "silent," "beautiful," and "dead" written on it. She didn't remember writing that. The words, she knew, came from the Chief Seattle speech Nana had made her memorize as a little girl; the speech had been circulating through her thoughts all morning:

> *...when the streets of your cities and villages shall be silent, and you think them deserted, they will throng with the returning hosts that once filled and still love this beautiful land. The white man will never be alone. Let him be just and deal kindly with my people, for the dead are not altogether powerless...*

The speech, Nana had insisted, would give Kiki a sense of pride in her family's past. But that wasn't what it felt like now. As she looked out at the rain, the words sounded more like the eulogy of a dying people and not the pronouncement of an imminent rebirth. The dead held no power. And her grandma was not among some "returning host" ready to demand justice. There was only loss. Yet here she sat, adrift within that loss, a microfilm machine glowing a pale gray in front of her. She had been at the library for some two hours going through newspapers from around the time of the brothel ledger entries. The previous day's excitement at finding the names had faded. She had about ten more minutes before she needed to catch the bus up to the hospital to start work. But whether it was ten minutes or two hours, it didn't matter. The burden of all the dead, not just her grandmother, weighed her down as ancestral ghosts hovered at the edges of her perception.

The microfilm machine displayed the front page of a nineteenth-century newspaper. With a quarter twist of the advance-image knob, a new page from the *Seattle Weekly Gazette* slid into view. Kiki had started with newspapers dated a little before the time her mother's namesake disappeared from the brothel. She was nearly a year out now. Still nothing.

Kiki did a quick scan of the image on the screen, brushing past the barrage of ads for hotels, clothing stores, and various Seattle bars and breweries claiming to have the city's best liquors and cigars. She was about to forward to the next page when she spotted a small news brief in the lower left column titled "Indian Found Dead." The short, six-line article didn't elicit much of a reaction until she reached the fourth line, which listed the name Reuben Furth. And maybe it was the near-desperate need to find something relevant, but she immediately felt certain this was the same man listed in the brothel leger.

The article stated that Mr. Furth was the one who found the body of the dead Indian woman. There was no name given for the woman. No description. Only that Mr. Furth had found her outside of his residence, her face badly swollen and bruised from what the article described as injuries from a fall.

Kiki scanned ahead to look for a follow-up article. Nothing.

In her notebook, she copied down each word of the article, underlining the man's name and the article's publication date. But as she wrote these things down, an uneasy feeling settled over her. This was him; she felt certain of that; but the initial excitement of the discovery was changing into something else. Distress, maybe. Fear. If this was the Rueben from the ledger, did that make the dead woman her mother's namesake? That seemed absurd, though; the idea that the woman in the article was Kiki's great-great-great grandmother. And what about the cause of death? It rang false, she thought. The wounds sounded as if someone had beaten the woman to death. The article made no mention of a child, either. If this was her ancestral grandmother, there needed to be a child.

Kiki looked at her watch. She was going to be late for work. She made a note to check the other Seattle newspapers around this same date to look for additional information. She toyed with the idea of calling in sick to continue the research. But there would be time to come back tomorrow. If there was more to find out, it wasn't going to go anywhere in the next twenty-four hours.

Friday

Pain radiated from the soles of Clay's feet. He rolled to his side and tried to coax himself back to sleep even though he wasn't all that certain he had ever gone to sleep at all. Far too early to get up, he thought. The throb of discomfort intensified, forcing him to turn on the bedside light. Drawing back the covers, he found streaks of red staining the lower half of the sheets. The combination of alcohol, benzos, and sleeping pills clouded his thoughts and made it difficult to process the blood. The pain he understood. But it took a moment to recognize the blood and the fact that it had come from his feet. Scratches covered the palms of his hands. There was dirt compacted under his nails.

To his left, the alarm clock read 2:49 a.m.

He moved to the side of the bed and set his feet on the floor. His first attempt to stand failed as pain shot through his body and sent him collapsing backwards.

"Fuck!" The snap sound of the obscenity rang hollow in the small room.

On the next try, he put the weight on the sides of his feet and managed to hobble to the bathroom. Spots of dried blood dotted the carpet, starting at the front door and heading into the bedroom.

He had been out wandering. No point to pretend otherwise, not with the pain and the blood.

Taking up a bottle of hydrogen peroxide and a wad of gauze, he sat on the toilet and applied the acidic liquid to the cuts on his hands and feet. Tiny, fizzing bubbles overflowed each of the wounds, the rush of pain further clearing his chemically muddled thoughts. Despite the thick calluses on his feet, there were several sizable gashes. In those deeper wounds, once the peroxide bubbles subsided, he took a pair of tweezers and probed each one to make sure there were no splinters or thorns that might cause infection.

Finished, he reclined against the tank of the toilet, exhausted by the pain. His hands shook, and his stomach felt tight with nausea. There were vague memories of digging in the muddy earth, his feet being cut along a sharp-rocked path. The smell of the Puget Sound and the wet night air. Images of shallow swampy water. Blood. But not from his feet. Not his blood at all.

Lifting his left foot, he took a clean piece of toilet paper and pressed it against the largest of the wounds, holding it there, applying more pressure until a delirious flood of pain filled his head and pushed aside further thoughts of blood and water. He then stood and turned on the shower. The old steel pipes rattled to life as water spat from the mineral-stained shower nozzle. He grabbed nail clippers and took a seat on the side of the tub and scraped, trimmed, and filed his dirty, jagged fingernails. The rhythmical sound of the water pattered against the iron tub, permeating the space, offering up a calming distraction against the jumbled images of the night's meandering.

Standing, he stripped off the muddy clothes and climbed into the steaming shower. Eyes closed, he let the scalding-hot water wash over him.

Early Morning

At first, Kiki wondered if her eyes were open, such was the near-perfect darkness of the bedroom. Then came the noise. Again. Like a footstep. Like someone walking across the apartment's wooden floors, the sounds moving in the direction of her bedroom. A sliver of gray light filtered in from the living room. A stirring of movement appeared at the edge of the doorframe; and within that fractured instant, her dreaming mind bloomed into frightened consciousness as a shadowed figure glided into the bedroom. It was hard to breathe, and her heart felt about to explode from her chest. Then the creak of the old floorboards sounded at the foot of her bed, the cadence rising and falling with the rhythm of someone carefully moving through the ink-black darkness. For a moment, the room went quiet. Then came the sound of something being removed from the top of the dresser. A necklace, maybe. She struggled to stay still, struggled to see something, to contain the urge to leap out of bed and run for the apartment door. She wanted to scream. Couldn't open her mouth. She would have cried, but her body had all but shut down.

And in that silence, she heard breathing, a labored breathing, like an animal in pain. The heavy scent of rain permeated the room. There was a shift of weight and the footsteps moved back in the direction of the bedroom door, the ghost-like shape gliding out and into the living room. She strained to follow the sounds, praying he was moving towards the apartment door. The awful pounding of her heart grew painful, making it difficult to hear anything. Floorboards creaked not far from the bedroom, as if the intruder had stopped at the dining room table. She then heard one of the stacks of research material tumbling to the floor. The trembling of her body made the bed begin to squeak. The footsteps resumed. Slowly. There was no hurry to the steps as they moved to the far end of the apartment. Then came the soft tick-tick-tick of the apartment door's brass hinges being slowly opened and then just as slowly closed. A quiet click sounded as the door latched shut. But she still couldn't move. All she needed to do was make it to the phone out in the living room and call the police. All she needed to do was get up and lock the door, push the couch against the door and call the police. But her body refused to do anything but shake.

Friday

An intense chill hung in the winter air as Clay approached the Madison Park apartment building where his mother lived. The cuts on his feet forced a slight limp. It was around ten o'clock in the morning. He had planned to visit Eva's place earlier, but Melissa had wanted an update on the story he had scheduled for tomorrow's paper. On top of that, Detective Carpenter had called to discuss the statistics story and confirm the drive-along for later that night. Clay hadn't needed a reminder. Not with the dread he felt about spending more time with the detective, who was sure to find new ways of making him uncomfortable. The delays along with the detective's call had irritated him and further soured his mood.

Eva, fortunately, would still be asleep. He could count on that. If he was quick and quiet, he could pick up the family papers and photographs without the hassle of answering any questions.

At the building's security door, he briefly wondered if maybe he should wake Eva up once he had the material and talk to her about the night wanderings, the dreams. She might be able help, he thought. But he knew Eva. And he knew she would make assumptions and talk over the top of him; and in the end, he would snap at her for not listening, and the visit would culminate with the two of them arguing. He pushed the black call button for apartment 401. Unlike most of the other apartments, there was no name next to the number.

"The only people who need to know I live here are the people who already know," Eva had stated on more than one occasion.

A police siren started up nearby.

As he waited a few moments to make sure his mother wasn't awake, Clay shifted his weight from one foot to the other to temper the discomfort in his feet. She wouldn't be awake, though. He knew that. She was still asleep, and the weak buzz of the intercom would never be loud enough to get her up. Without bothering to push the button again, he took out his set of Eva's apartment keys and unlocked the front security door.

Reaching the fourth floor, he used the keys again to open the door for apartment 401. It opened into a small entryway. A geometric-patterned Navajo rug hung on the wall to the right and an out-of-focus, black-and-white photograph of a nude woman posed near a small pond hung on the left. At the end of the hallway was Eva's bedroom. The soft rattle of someone snoring, along with the low chatter of television voices, came from the room. Eva had fallen asleep with the TV on, no doubt staying up until three or four in the morning watching old movies and drinking gin and tonics. And there would be a snack plate next to the bed with leftover Swiss cheese and saltine crackers. It was a scene he had witnessed countless times while growing up.

Clay took a left past the bedroom and made his way towards the kitchen and living room. If he remembered correctly, the material he wanted would be in one of the bookcases in the living room. But as he walked down the short hallway, an unpleasant odor of stale liquor and garbage intensified. Upon reaching the kitchen, he stopped. The scale of the mess in that small space left him slack. Eva had never been much of a housekeeper. This, however, was something else. He had expected a few dirty dishes and maybe a trash bag to take down to the dumpster. Not this, though. He leaned against the doorframe, feeling more exhausted than ever. Garbage spilled from the trashcan in the left corner of the kitchen. The smoldering mess included glass beer and liquor bottles, Styrofoam take-out containers, and store-bought food boxes and cans. Dirty dishes overflowed the sink and surrounding countertop. The smell. It reminded him of the Nichols brothers' house and the noxious odor of death and decay.

His first thought was to grab what he needed and leave. No one would know he had been there. Certainly not Eva, who continued to snore away in the bedroom, sleeping off the previous night's alcohol. There had been times like this growing up where her drinking had taken over and left the rest of her life to rot like the garbage in front of him. It seemed like it had been a while, though. At least what he could remember. But it may have been around for some time since he hadn't seen her in a while.

He took a tentative step into the kitchen with the idea of picking up the trash. But only the trash, he thought. This wasn't his mess. He did a quick search of the cupboards for more garbage bags, but only found an empty box. That left him to wrestle free the bag buried beneath the pile of garbage, creating an avalanche of bottles and take-out containers that spread the debris further across the floor. Using his foot as a press, he made more room in the bag; a foul brown liquid began to leak from a rip in the bottom. After adding more garbage, Clay picked the bag up and hustled it from the apartment, down the stairs and outside to the back alleyway where several dumpsters sat next to the building. A sour-smelling, syrupy liquid coated his hands and shirt as he emptied out the trash in order to reuse the bag.

Back in the kitchen, he picked up more waste and hauled it down to the dumpsters, repeating this process two more times before clearing out all the garbage. After the last trip, he found a mop wedged between the refrigerator and the wall and wiped up the slick of brown sludge on the kitchen floor. His head felt a little clearer from the exertion of going up and down the stairs so many times.

Next came the dishes. The more he cleaned, the calmer he felt; he had stopped dwelling on the reason he had come to Eva's in the first place.

The apartment went quiet once he finished the dishes and turned the water off. Eva's snoring had stopped. Clay listened, waiting to hear a sound or movement. Nothing came. Anxious that she might be awake, he went into the living room and searched the two bookcases for the old family photos and assorted documents. Nothing. He looked through every photo album, but none of them went back more than fifty or sixty years. The material he wanted was more than a hundred years old.

The calm of a few minutes ago began to shift back to a feeling of agitation and anxiety. He headed to Eva's bedroom. At the door, he could see her on her side, her eyes a quarter of the way open. She was breathing. Her barely open eyes, though, had a lost look about them as if she were trying to figure out where she was. Clay entered the room; the sounds on the television served to mask his movements. A plate with cracker crumbs sat on the far side of the bed and a nearly empty bottle of gin and a tumbler-sized glass occupied the nightstand. He scanned a bookshelf near the window. Little piles of this and that were scattered around the room. He picked through those, then carefully opened the closet and began to search the upper shelves. Still nothing.

Eva's eyes had opened a little wider. She looked awake. Lost, but awake. If he asked for help, she would have questions about why he wanted these items. He didn't want to answer any questions. But the search of the room turned up nothing. He had put this off too long, and it couldn't wait any longer.

Unwilling to leave empty handed, he crouched down next to the bed. "Mom?" She didn't respond. He raised his voice a little. "Mom?" When she looked at him, her expression remained puzzled. Her breath smelled of stale liquor.

"Can you hear me?"

Her voice crackled with a mix of confusion and annoyance. "What ... what are you doing here?"

"Just a visit to see how you're doing," he lied.

"What time is it?"

Clay looked at his watch, surprised that it was already past eleven. He had been here for more than an hour. "Almost eleven-thirty," he said.

"Eleven? Why are you here so early?"

The response produced a wry smile and made Clay wish he had left rather than wake her up. "I'm looking for something."

"You know better than to show up this early?"

"It's almost noon. That isn't early. But that's fine, I'll come back." He straightened up.

"Oh, stop that," she said with an irritated wave of her arm. "Give me a second to wake up and get dressed. Go on. Go! I'll be out in a moment."

Should have left, he thought. He could feel that now as he exited the room.

"Could you get some coffee going, please?" Eva shouted after him.

Coffee. Of course.

In the kitchen, he opened the lid of the coffee maker and took out the used filter, quickly realizing he had thrown out the trash bag with the last trip to the dumpsters and had nowhere to put the soggy mess. He placed it in the sink. Next, he searched the cupboards for coffee and a clean filter.

"Where's the coffee?" he shouted after coming up empty.

"What?"

45

"Coffee? Filters? Where?"

A mumbled response followed that sounded like "in the bottom drawer." Clay checked the kitchen drawers, eventually finding the items on the Lazy Susan in the cupboard next to the sink.

Eva shuffled into the kitchen a few minutes later still looking half-asleep. She was dressed in khaki-colored cotton pants and an orange-flowery blouse. The clinking of metal and wood followed her as half a dozen colored bracelets sounded with the movements of her arms.

"Tough night?" Clay asked.

"Don't start." She attempted to clear her throat several times. From the mound of dishes drying across the counter, she grabbed a cup and then pulled out the coffee pot, some of the still-brewing liquid spilling on the warming plate. She didn't seem to take any notice of the vastly altered state of the kitchen. With the coffee cup in hand, she went and sat on one of the chairs in the living room. Clay poured a cup of his own and took a seat on the couch across from her.

After several sips of the black coffee, a bit of color returned to Eva's tired face. "That's better," she said and cleared her throat once more. "When you make coffee, though, you need to make it a lot stronger. I'll have to brew another pot just to get through the day."

"I'm sorry, was that a thank you?"

"You woke me up, remember."

"True enough. I should know better." Clay looked down at the black liquid surface of the coffee and warned himself to be careful not to say something hateful. He felt in that kind of mood. He didn't like it, didn't like the swirl of feelings that had settled over him.

"What did you say you were here for?" she asked. "And, by the way, you're looking more than a little rough around the edges yourself. Is everything all right?"

Clay's hands rubbed against the smooth surface of the warm cup as if the movement and heat might end the conversation sooner. "I'm fine, I guess." He paused a moment, debating whether to add anything about his sleeping issues. "I've started sleepwalking again," he said, looking down.

A bit of Eva's energy seemed to dissipate. "What makes you think you're sleepwalking?" The question came out as both an inquiry and an accusation, as if she were searching for a reason not to believe him.

He thought about taking off his shoes and showing her the cuts on his feet. That might be enough to avoid an elaborate explanation.

"Well?" Eva asked impatiently.

"When I wake up," he said, "my clothes are wet, and I don't remember going outside." He stopped there, despite the urge to say more. What would she say about the blood? Or the dreams? The people's faces?

Eva, however, didn't seem to notice his apprehension, her eyes fixed on the curtained living room windows. "Have you seen a doctor?" she asked.

"I have. No one gives me a straight answer, though. What did we do when I was younger?"

"I don't know," Eva said. "We talked to so many different people and tried so many different treatments."

Unsure of what to do with his hands, Clay leaned forward and put the coffee cup on the table. "It would help if you could remember something." He did his best to steady his voice, to avoid an impatient or angry tone.

"At one point, I put a lock on the outside of your bedroom door," she said. "I remember that much. That seemed to work as well as anything."

"A lock?" Clay tried to laugh, but the sound came out as a clipped grunt. "I'd forgotten about that."

"The lock was a last resort after you got hurt," she said. "I didn't know what else to do."

"Hurt?" But even as the question left his mouth, he understood what she was talking about.

47

"When you broke your arm and ankle. You do remember that, don't you?

"Yes," he nodded.

"I still have nightmares about getting that call at two in the morning from the police telling me my twelve-year-old son, who I thought was asleep in bed, was actually in the emergency room."

"I get it!" He didn't want to talk about this anymore. What he remembered, what he allowed himself to remember, was waking up in the hospital. It was never clear how he broke his arm and ankle. A car might have hit him, one doctor guessed, or he could have fallen from somewhere high, like a roof.

"That was about the time your father and I were getting divorced," Eva said. She brought her coffee cup up but stopped halfway before taking a drink. "Not a very pleasant year, as I recall."

"All I want to know," Clay said, "is did the doctors prescribe any specific medications? Did they recommend any treatments?"

"There were a couple of medications, but I don't remember specifics," she said. "Most of the doctors seemed to think you'd grow out of it."

"That's it?" Emotion simmered at the edges of his unsteady voice.

"What are the doctors telling you now?" Eva asked.

"Nothing. They keep prescribing different sleeping pills, new anxiety medications, antipsychotics. I'm at the point where I never feel completely awake and never feel totally asleep."

"Do you go outside during these sleepwalking episodes?"

"Yes, I'm going outside! Are you not listening? I wake up wet. I wake up with dirt jammed deep under my fingernails. I have cuts on the bottom of my feet. Would you like to see the cuts?" He stopped himself, though, because he was about to tell her about the dreams and the blood that filled his memories of those dreams.

"Calm down, Clay. I'm only trying to understand what's going on with you."

He took a deep breath, but it was hard with his chest so tight. "Sorry. I'm a little tired." But the words were a lie; sleep wasn't going to solve his problems. "I didn't come here to talk about the sleepwalking, though. I'm looking for great-great-great-grandfather's photo albums and family documents. I thought you kept those things out here in the bookcases."

"I moved that stuff out a while ago. What do you need it for?"

"Does it matter?"

"Yes, it matters..."

"Research. I'm doing some family research. Can you tell me where it is?"

Eva took a drink of coffee and offered an indifferent shrug. "It's in a box somewhere."

"Okay. Where should I start looking?" Clay could feel his veneer of patience slipping away.

"I'll have to think about it. What happened to that last box of stuff I gave you?"

This back-and-forth between himself and Eva felt very familiar. But not in a pleasant way. "Still looking through it," he lied. It was all gone. Burned. The same thing he wanted to do with the photos and documents. "Is it in your apartment storage unit in the basement?"

"Could be."

He didn't have a key to that. "Do you mind if I go and look?"

"Yes, I mind. Give me a day or two and I'll go through it."

The room went quiet. Clay closed his eyes, resisting the impulse to get up and bully Eva into giving him the storage unit key. He needed to get this bullshit over with; he had already waited too long and knew it would be a

49

mistake to put it off any longer. But he needed to avoid an argument with Eva; this would not be the last of his visits. "Did you notice the kitchen?" he asked with a frustrated tremble in his voice.

"Yes. I was going to get to it today. You're not the only one with things going on, Clay."

"You mean you don't have time between your drinking and ordering take-out. Is that what you have going on?"

"Stop! There's nothing wrong with my drinking. And I certainly don't need any lectures from you."

Clay stood up. It was time to leave. He would have to come back. He could feel his anger rising, and things would only get worse if he stayed.

"Next time, I'll let you clean up that mound of garbage!"

"I didn't ask for help. If I need help from you, I'll come knocking on your door at four in the morning and wake you up. Deal?"

Friday Night

The words on the medical chart blurred to the point of being unreadable as Kiki's thoughts returned to the silhouette that had moved through her bedroom early that morning. She had asked the floor supervisor for the day off. He had said no. The unit was already short staffed. If she could walk and didn't have a fever over 102, he had said, she needed to come in. Maybe it was better this way. Being at work. At least here, she knew people and felt a little less vulnerable.

The police certainly hadn't helped to make her feel safe. It took an officer more than three hours to arrive at her apartment. By then, the morning sun had begun to lighten the eastern sky. And her emotional state had shifted from frightened to angry. She demanded to know why it took so long for someone to show up.

"Calls are prioritized based on the immediacy of the emergency," the officer had explained with a tone of indifference. "It's been a busy morning."

The officer then spent about five minutes questioning her and glancing around the apartment. It left her feeling as if he didn't believe her, as if she were lying about the break-in.

"All that's missing are a couple of pieces of jewelry?" the officer asked. "Do you have pictures of these items?"

"The pieces were family heirlooms. I'll have to do a little searching to find a photograph."

"What about the value?"

"I don't know. One was a gold ring with a small diamond. The other one was silver."

"There's no sign of forced entry. Anyone else have a key: an old boyfriend, other family members, a neighbor?"

"No, no one else has a key." Between the officer's skeptical tone and her own vague memories, she wondered if she had dreamed parts of what had happened, perhaps misplacing the jewelry instead of having it stolen. She thought to check the floor around the dresser to make sure it hadn't fallen off. The worst part, the thing that made her sick to her stomach, was the fact Nana had given her both those pieces of jewelry; it felt like she had lost another part of her grandmother.

"Did the intruder make any physical contact with you?"

Again, she replied no. This whole process, she realized, was going nowhere. She had nothing to indicate a burglary other than she had seen the outline of someone come into her room, or thought she had seen someone come in. It started to sound as crazy as calling her grandmother's death a homicide.

The officer said he would file a report, but without a picture of the stolen items, or a description of the intruder, there was very little the police department could do for her.

Fever. Trouble breathing. Dehydration. These words rose from the flurry of letters and lines on the medical chart. She wrote down the time, 5:35 p.m. She filled in the appropriate boxes with the patient's vital signs. She then felt for a pulse on the underside of the man's wrist and started to count while looking at the second hand on her watch. She added that information to the sheet.

Her movements had a mechanicalness about them that offered the appearance of normalcy. No one at work had noticed anything unusual. No one had asked if anything was wrong. She was a quiet person anyway. So the fact that she hadn't engaged in any of the never-ending workplace gossip wasn't seen as unusual. Yet on the inside, she felt frantic, overwhelmed by a building emotional pressure that verged on the catastrophic.

"How are you feeling," she started and then looked back at the chart for the man's name, "Mr. George?"

The elderly man had an oxygen mask over his face. His eyes were open, but he didn't respond to her question.

"Mr. George?"

The man looked in her direction and nodded as if finally becoming aware of her presence.

"How are you feeling?"

"Fine," came the man's muffled response.

Kiki noted that in the chart. "Do you want to try to eat something?"

The man shook his head no.

Before coming to work, Kiki had called her friend, Melanie, and had left a message about the break-in, asking if it was possible to stay at her place tonight. She hadn't heard back. She needed to call again. She didn't want to return to her own apartment. Not right now. Maybe by tomorrow she would feel better. Maybe. It didn't seem possible. But time had a strange way of making even the most horrific experiences more tolerable.

Kiki adjusted Mr. George's bedding and gently touched the elderly man's shoulder. "My name is Kiki. Let me know if you need anything. I'll be here until midnight."

Friday Night

Western Avenue traffic had transitioned from rush-hour, single-occupant commuters to couples driving somewhere for a night out: dinner, the theater, a concert, a friend's party, etc. Somewhere distracting. Somewhere bright and welcoming. Clay watched them go by, occasionally glancing west at the faint outline of Myrtle Edwards Park and then towards Elliot Bay and the white lights of the ferries traveling across the Sound to Bremerton and Bainbridge Island. Several blocks away, the neon glow of the newspaper's globe cast a surreal set of blue, red, and gold colors against the darkened sky. Rain pattered away on the hood of Clay's jacket. Looking up, he saw drops of water materialize out of the dark night and into the washed-out gray glimmer of the ambient streetlights. There was no party for Clay. No concert. No dinner date. The night would consist of his morbid thoughts and the growl of Detective Carpenter's voice. The detective, of course, was late. He had agreed to pick Clay up at seven. It was now seven twenty-two. Ten more minutes, he thought. He would give the detective ten more minutes. After that, he would head home, a prospect that further antagonized his dark mood. He dreaded the hollow silence of the apartment, becoming locked away with his thoughts that would obsess over the need to return to Eva's to collect the family documents; the filth of Eva's apartment; the foul smells and leaking trash bag; the inevitability of sleep and the expectation of rising and wandering around in a state half-awake, half-dead.

And so despite the aggravation, he continued to wait for the detective, the same man who treated him like a child when it came to the city's violence. He had tried to tell the detective he had dealt with this sort of thing before, but the detective declined to listen. One event in particular stood out as a good illustration of this experience; it occurred when he had worked as a reporter in north-central Idaho; the sheriff's department had allowed him to follow along on a meth lab bust. The raid centered on a doublewide mobile home situated at the end of an isolated gravel road within the Nez Perce Reservation. He stood a hundred yards back as law enforcement surrounded the run-down structure. The deputy at the lead of the battering ram knocked twice, identified himself, and then destroyed the front door with the black metal tube. Officers stormed into the house in a flurry of bellowing energy that lasted but a few moments. The world went suddenly quiet, like a door slamming shut. A deputy came out of the house shouting for someone to get medical help. Clay moved closer to the shabby mobile home. The faces of the officers leaving the residence had a pained, sallow appearance. One deputy got sick as he exited the trailer. And as Clay entered through the front door, he saw several men huddled over a crib in the far-left corner of the living room. On a couch, a few yards from the front door, sprawled the unmoving body of an emaciated woman. An officer had a man pinned to the floor and was applying handcuffs. The man's eyes were open, but there was a glassy appearance to them, as if he did not understand where he was or what was happening. An overpowering smell of noxious chemicals strafed the air. At the crib, an officer picked up the form of a small baby; its thin arms sagged lifelessly at its side, the skin as white as the afternoon clouds dotting the sky.

An unsettling mix of excitement and horror had surged through Clay's head as he watched the scene unfold. He barely remembered returning to the newsroom later in the day to write the story. Could only recall bits and pieces of the next week as he did additional reporting for a longer follow-up article that took up most of the Sunday paper. Those articles ended up winning several journalism awards and were one of the reasons he had gotten his current job. But the experience hung at the back of his head like a festering wound, both for how it sickened him and for the strange rush of exhilaration it brought – not unlike his reaction at the Nichols brothers' house.

With his eyes closed, Clay tilted his head back and let the rain tap against his face, each drop a small sting on his cold skin. The trip to the Nichols' house had brought out other memories, too. Familial memories. Memories of violence he didn't want to acknowledge as his own. That included the night he had been injured, the one his mom had talked about earlier in the day. He had broken into a house that night. The injuries had resulted from him jumping out a second-story window.

The loud blast of a car horn rousted him back from the rain, and he saw the detective's unmarked sedan pulling up next to the curb.

"What the hell are you doing?" Detective Carpenter shouted through the open passenger window. "You looked like a goddamned statue."

"I'm just patiently waiting for you," Clay said. A wall of hot air greeted him as he stepped out of the rain and into the car. The heat gave the car an uncomfortably humid feel.

"Blame my ex-wife for the wait. I was having a come-to-Jesus conversation with her about my girls."

"And how did that go?"

56

"As expected, she hung up on me and then wouldn't answer the phone when I called back. You know anything about teenage girls?"

"No."

"I don't claim to know much, but my ex-wife seems to know even less. The girls do whatever they want, wear whatever they want, and their mother doesn't seem to care."

"And what horrific things are your daughters up to?"

"First of all, my girls are fifteen and twelve and they dress and act like they're thirty and ready to work the streets. And that doesn't seem to bother my ex. In fact, she's the one buying the tight, inappropriate clothes and god-awful makeup." The detective took a left and gave a sharp curse under his breath. "You want some advice?"

"About teenage girls? Not really."

"Don't get married. Women are crazy. I love my two girls, but I can see the crazy growing in them by the second."

"I'll keep that in mind," Clay said in an uninterested tone. The cuts on his feet throbbed from standing so long at the corner.

"...ready to have fun."

"Fun?"

The detective grinned. "We're meeting with some old friends who should be able to give me some answers on the double homicide."

"Why do I have the feeling your 'friends' are going to be less than excited to see you."

"Nonsense. They love me like the father they never had."

The rain streaked across the passenger-side window, the moist warmth of the car beginning to melt into Clay's skin. "And where are we meeting these friends?"

"Since it's Friday, we'll start the search at a dark little hole near Pioneer Square."

After several turns, the detective had them heading south along First Avenue. The traffic grew heavier as cars filed into the nightclub- and bar-heavy area around Pioneer Square.

"Did you grow up in Seattle?" Clay asked as they waited at another stoplight. He wanted to move his thoughts away from Eva and the host of other mental irritants.

"Nope. Born and bred in beautiful West Oakland."

"What brought you here?"

The detective gave Clay a look that made it clear this was the last of the personal questions he would answer. "After my second tour in Nam, I was discharged out of Fort Lewis. The Seattle Police Department had openings. I applied. I got hired. Not much more complicated than that. Now, we're coming up on our first stop of the night."

"A frat bar in Pioneer Square?"

"Not quite. We're going farther south."

The detective continued through Pioneer Square and traveled a couple of more minutes before pulling up across from what appeared to be an area of abandoned warehouses. With the car parked beneath one of the few working streetlamps in the area, Clay watched as ghost-like shadows flitted at the edges of the light, shifting with the evening's wind and rain.

"Who are we looking for?"

The detective gazed into the semi-darkened alley between two of the warehouses. "Over there. About halfway down. There's a small group I'm hoping will give me some direction on the murders."

Clay followed the detective's eyes but failed to see anything but vague outlines. "We're going in the alley?"

"Relax," the detective said. "Just stay close to me."

"And if something happens?"

"You know how to run, don't you?" The detective smiled. "It'll be fine. Besides, these boys will be excited to see me. And let me remind you, you are here as my guest and not a reporter covering a story. Is there any confusion on that?"

"I get it."

"Don't give me that 'I get it' bullshit. Things might get a little unorthodox, and I need to know this won't end up in Monday's paper. Are we clear on that?"

"Yes, we're clear."

The detective shot Clay one final warning glance, then opened his door and stepped into the drizzly night. Clay followed, not entirely sure what he had just agreed to. It certainly was not his habit to give up his ability to write about something. There were more things at work here than a single story, though.

The two men crossed the street, the sound of their footsteps blending with the rain. No other cars were around.

"Stay to my right," the detective said. "If things start to get heated, don't run. I was kidding about running. If you run, that will only get these boys more excited. We'll back away if needed. But no running."

Clay wondered if this was another of the detective's jokes. But there was no humor in the man's broad face. "Right. No running."

"Better yet," the detective corrected himself, "since my supervisor doesn't know you're here, if we start to back away just get behind me. It's best if you don't get shot. And at no point are you to talk, especially if someone asks you a question or pokes fun at you or tries to goad you into getting angry."

"Sure."

It was then that Clay saw the group midway down the alley, barely visible in the gray city light. The detective stopped at the mouth of the foul-smelling passageway, his black skin blending with the surrounding darkness. Voices swirled in time with the rhythm of the rain. It sounded like several of the men were arguing. Clay took a step forward to get a better view, but the detective motioned him back. The group of about a dozen people congregated beneath an overhang from one of the warehouse's side doorways. After a few moments of assessment, the detective approached the group. He did not attempt to be quiet, nor did he stay to the shadows, choosing instead to walk straight down the middle of the puddle-filled alleyway. A figure at the edge of the semicircle was the first to notice him and hushed the raised voices. Within seconds, a whispered quiet settled over the group. Several individuals turned and headed to the adjoining street at the other end of the alley.

Clay's breathing grew tight and shallow. The sound and clarity of the rain intensified and the movement of each member of the group registered with an unnatural crispness. He tried not to focus on the fear, or the myriad things that could go wrong. He wanted to experience the rush of it. Not the violence. But the thrill.

A figure against to the warehouse wall stepped out. "What the hell you want, old man?"

The individual wore a dark rain jacket, the hood pulled over his head, obscuring most of his facial features except the outline of a square jaw. He was tall, maybe six foot two. His shoulders had a forward roll like a boxer's, or that of an angry dog tensed for a fight.

"Relax, Justin," the detective responded in a surprisingly calm tone. "We haven't talked in a while and I wanted to check in to see how things were going with you. How's your mom and sister doing?"

Seven people stood in front of the detective and Clay. Most remained under the corrugated overhang. They all had their hands inside of pants or jacket pockets; each appeared a little uncertain on whether to run or fight. "I don't know anyone named Justin, old man."

The detective responded with a deep laugh. "No, I'm pretty sure it's Justin. That's the name I've booked you under since you were eight years old."

"Redman," the hooded figure stated and spat in the direction of the detective's shoes. "The name is Redman. Justin is a slave's name. And unlike you, old man, I'm nobody's slave."

"Oh, right. Let me see if I remember correctly: your great-great-great-grandfather was a Buffalo soldier who married a Sioux maiden. Did I get that right? Or was she a princess?"

"What the fuck you want?"

The detective moved under the shelter of the overhang and motioned for Clay to follow.

"Scoot over, friend," he ordered one of the other figures huddled under the small roof. "Keep scooting." The detective then motioned with his hand until the man stood in the rain. "There you go. You've got the smell of someone who needs a good shower. Now, Justin, before I ask everyone to empty out their pockets, I have a couple of questions I need you to answer. If you give me straight and truthful responses, I'll leave without any further interruption to your night. Do you understand what I'm saying? Do you need me to repeat any of that?"

"What's your question?"

The rain pinged on the metal roof like falling nails.

"The shooting last week. The two brothers."

Redman shrugged. "What about it?"

"A couple of your friends told me you know something about it."

"Not true."

"I also heard you went by the Nichols brothers' house earlier that night."

This time Redman broke into a laugh. "Hell I did."

"I have witnesses that say differently."

"No, you don't. And if you do, they're full of shit."

"I've got sworn testimony. In fact, I have more than enough to arrest you right now and let you rot downtown for the next couple of weeks. But, seeing how we're such good friends, I want to give you a chance to tell me what you know about the shooting?"

"Nothing. That's what I know."

"That's too bad." The detective picked at a fingernail on his left hand. "I'm taking a lot of heat right now from my superiors and I need to show some progress on this case. And you, my brother, are my lead suspect."

"Suspect? Your mind is getting soft, old man. I wasn't anywhere near that fucking place. I have a rock-solid alibi."

"Really? I've got an equally solid set of witnesses telling me those two brothers owed you money. A lot of money. So there's motive. I have another witness who puts you in that area around the time of the shooting. There's opportunity. And I bet if I did a search of your home, I'd find a gun with your prints on it that would miraculously match the one used as the murder weapon. So let me rephrase the question so that it is easier for your muddled head to comprehend: Who shot the Nichols brothers? That's all I need to know. Not too difficult. You tell me that and I leave you all in peace to further squander your short lives."

Redman took a step towards the detective. "I'm not telling you shit, Uncle T—"

Before Redman could finish the sentence, however, the detective hit him with a backhand to the side of the face. Redman stumbled out into the rain. Several of the figures standing on the perimeter either looked away or brought a hand to their mouths to stifle bursts of surprised laughter.

The detective moved to within a foot of a fuming Redman. "I want a name. And if the name doesn't check out, I'm coming back later tonight with some off-duty friends to clean up this shit-hole alley. And I'm not talking about emptying out pockets at this point."

With his eyes locked on the detective, Redman slowly wiped away a bit of blood that had come from his nose.

"Go fuck yourself!" Then his hand made a quick movement as if to take a swing. The detective seemed to anticipate this, took an even quicker step forward, and slammed an open palm to Redman's face, the force of the blow dropping him to the black-graveled alleyway.

The detective then knelt, planting a heavy knee on Redman's chest, reached into the man's jacket, and brought out a small handgun. "I expected a little better of you, Justin. This is what you didn't want to do." The detective then pointed at one of the tense figures standing in the rain. "What's your name, son?"

The man straightened. "Nate."

"I should have known that. We've met." The detective smiled and turned back to Redman, who appeared to have a difficult time breathing under the weight. "See how nicely Nate responded to my question, Justin? That was all you had to do. Now, Nate, if you thought that last hit was funny, watch this." The detective drew back his arm and backhanded Redman to the side of the face. "Now that is funny," the detective said in a flat, angry tone. For the others standing around, the surprised amusement of a moment ago had ceased.

The detective leaned over and put his face in front of Redman. "You want to try taking a swing at me now, boy?" the detective asked.

Redman shook his head, his hands ineffectively pushing against the detective's knee.

"Are you going to answer my questions?"

Redman offered a grunt that the detective seemed to take as a yes.

"Good. Let's get you off that cold, wet pavement." The detective stood. He offered a hand to Redman but the other man, still trying to catch his breath, knocked it away as he raised himself to a sitting position.

The detective turned and assessed each of the figures who formed the loose semi-circle. "You okay over there, Clay?"

Clay nodded, his mouth too dry to speak. His fists were clenched, and every muscle in his body had tensed up as if he were about to jump into the violence.

"Nate, what about you? You all right?" The detective's voice had a dark, irritated pitch to it. "I want you to stay alert because I am about to knock a baseball-sized blood clot from Justin's nose, and I don't want you to get hit in the face by it." And with that the detective took a handful of Redman's jacket and drew back a closed fist and looked about to swing forward, except this time Redman mumbled something.

"What's that?" the detective asked, hauling Redman to his feet.

Redman spoke several more unheard words, his head bowed and his eyes focused on a current of water running down the middle of the alley.

"Speak up, boy!" the detective said, his voice growing angrier.

"Watts," Redman repeated a little louder.

"Watts? Is that a name, or are you talking about a neighborhood in LA?"

"That's the name I've heard."

"First name, last name? Give me some damn direction!"

Redman took a deep breath and glanced up at the rain. Blood from his mouth ran down his chin and neck. "Don't know. That's all I've heard."

"Where do I find this Watts?"

Redman either did not answer or spoke so quietly that only the detective could hear him.

"What does he look like?"

"Don't know," Redman said with a shrug. "Some dude from Cali. That's all I've heard."

"That's not good enough, Justin." The detective raised his voice so everyone could hear him. "Because of my disappointment with Justin here, I want all of you to empty out your pockets. And I mean empty. If I find anything left in those baggy-ass pants, I'm locking you up for resisting."

Redman struggled to free himself from the detective's grip. "'Come on, man. I told you what I know…"

"Empty your goddamn pockets!" the detective shouted. "Everything! Now! Or I'm calling this in and booking all of you!"

By the time everyone emptied their pockets, the detective had a pile of cash and dozens of tiny ziplock bags half-filled with a white powder. The haul also included two guns and an assortment of knives, all of which the detective had put in his jacket pockets. "This could have all been avoided. All I wanted was a little cooperation. Clay, come over here and help me get rid of this shit."

The detective then began to stuff what must have been close to a thousand dollars in cash down a nearby storm drain. Next came the drugs. Clay and the detective carefully opened and then emptied each bag onto the wet asphalt. A chorus of complaints issued from the silhouetted figures up against the brick warehouse wall. None of them, however, moved.

Once all the drugs were gone, the detective stood up and seemed to consider something. "I'll be back tomorrow to repeat this," he said. "In fact, I'm going to keep coming back to track each of you down until one of you gives me something I can actually use. Understand? Am I making myself clear!" There were a few nods and mumbled responses. The detective continued to stare at the group before finally turning and heading back up the alley.

An adrenaline haze buzzed through Clay's head and a muscle-clenching tension suffused his body. He glanced back and saw the men continuing to glare at him and the detective. The hate in their faces was unmistakable. Their anger. This was not the end of the night for them, he knew.

Someone would have to answer for the lost cash and drugs.

"What a mess," the detective said once they were back in the car. "It's a good thing he said something because I was about to lose it. And I mean lose it. I was ready to hammer each one of those kids. Goddamn it!"

Water dripped from Clay's hair. His hand shook with an excited energy. "Did that name mean anything?" he asked, a little hesitant to speak given the detective's temper.

"I've heard it. Watts. Could be anything. A person. A gang. The thing that's got me so...I don't know." He took a deep breath. "I hate losing my control like that," he said, the tone of his voice leveling off. "Can't say I expected Justin to take a swing at me. That was the worst possible thing he could have done. He's lucky I stopped."

The detective stared in the direction of the alley as if expecting someone to emerge. He still hadn't started the car.

"So what's next?" Clay asked.

"A beer," the detective said. At that point, he put the keys in the ignition and brought the car to life. "Before that, I need to make a couple more stops. But you and I are done tonight. I'll drop you back at the paper."

Friday 1:15 a.m.

The nighttime glow of the city flickered in the windows of Melanie's third-floor apartment. The stop-and-go traffic of East Olive Way slowed and accelerated with the changing colors of the nearby stoplight. Across the street, a blue neon sign in the shape of a locomotive hung in the window of a coffee shop.

"Could it have been someone in the building?" she asked. She had a leg perched on the couch and faced Kiki as the two talked.

Kiki's eyes focused on the windows and the gray night beyond. "Maybe." She took a drink of wine. The harsh glare of the fluorescent kitchen light bathed the room in translucent shadows, transforming the red wine into something almost green. She was halfway done with her third glass. Only now was she starting to relax. When Kiki called from the hospital, Melanie had insisted she come over and stay the night even though it meant Kiki would arrive after midnight. The invitation came as a relief. She wouldn't have to go home. She wasn't sure when she would feel comfortable enough to go back.

"What about an old boyfriend? Or someone who knew about those pieces and what they meant to you?"

Kiki laughed. "I haven't dated anyone in more than a year. And no one other than you and a couple of coworkers have been to my apartment in recent months."

"You at least need to call the police again and get someone else to come out, especially if the first cop didn't believe you. That's ridiculous."

"It's understandable, I guess. The man didn't attack me or take anything valuable."

"I would still call again. Who knows what this asshole who broke in might try next? Anyway, you're welcome to stay here as long as you need to."

Kiki felt the truth of Melanie's words, and it helped her relax a little more. "Thank you." Her friendship with Melanie went back to grade school in West Seattle. Kiki felt a level of comfort with Melanie that was rare. And now that her grandmother was gone, there wasn't really anyone else.

"Why do you think he only took the necklaces?"

"It was a ring and two necklaces," Kiki said. She wasn't sure how much she wanted to tell Melanie about her theory surrounding Nana's death and the break-in. The whole thing, even to her, sounded crazy. The police thought so. And she was afraid Melanie would think she had lost it as well. "I'm not sure, really. My great-great-great-grandfather had owned the ring. The necklaces were from my great grandmother. It might have something to do with those family connections."

"See, I don't get that. Why would you risk breaking into someone's apartment and then only steal a couple of things that aren't worth much?"

Kiki finished the last bit of wine, picked up the bottle from the coffee table, and poured another full glass. "The officer asked that, too," Kiki responded. "I told him I thought the person who broke in was looking for those specific pieces. The guy went straight to the dresser where I put my jewelry at night. He didn't look anywhere else. It was like he knew what he wanted and where to find it." Kiki took another drink of wine. She wanted to tell Melanie the whole story, though. Melanie would understand, she thought. She needed someone to understand. "Did I ever talk to you about how Nana died? The cause of death?"

"You'd mentioned a heart attack, I think."

"The coroner listed that as the cause. But I think she died of something else."

Melanie refilled her own glass. "What do you mean?" A note of surprise had entered her voice.

Kiki then explained how Nana had never had heart problems. She told Melanie about the bloodshot eyes, Nana's nails, the threatening phone calls, all of it.

A look of disbelief spread across Melanie's face. "What do the police think?"

"That I'm crazy. They keep telling me that it all adds up to nothing more than random coincidences." Kiki looked at the dark liquid in her glass. She thought about the newspaper article on the murdered Indian woman. If she mentioned this to Melanie would it make her theory sound more reasonable or just further unbalanced?

"Okay," Melanie said. "But why would anyone want to hurt your grandmother? That doesn't make any sense."

Kiki watched the wine swirl around in small, uneven waves, thin legs of viscous liquid forming on the sides of the glass. Part of her regretted bringing any of this up. The deeper her explanation went, the more impossible it sounded. "Nana had been doing family research before she died. A lot of research. And it somehow seems like it's related to that." There, she had said it. Melanie was looking down now, though, like she didn't want to make eye contact.

"I can't imagine how hard it's been since your grandmother died. I know how close you two were. But this does sound a little crazy."

"I know." The sound of the nearby traffic filled the silence as the conversation trailed off. Kiki gave a hard swallow to hold back a cascade of emotions that threatened to break her calm exterior. Melanie was right. It was crazy. But if she stopped the search now, if she ignored her intuition and accepted her grandmother's death as a natural occurrence, the world, she feared, would slip away from her and leave her with nothing but loss and grief. She would give up at that point. She knew that. And so she reminded herself of the newspaper article that had mentioned Rueben and the dead Indian woman. Didn't that mean something? Wasn't that article more than just mere coincidence?

"Have you thought about seeing a therapist?" Melanie asked. "It might help if you could talk to someone. Get some help on how to process the loss of your grandma."

"Maybe," Kiki said. The softness of her voice made it sound as though she was talking to herself. "I pick up the phone sometimes and dial Nana's number. I listen to it ring, hoping she'll pick up and I'll hear her voice again."

Melanie moved next to Kiki and put an arm around her shoulder.

"The worst is that awful chiming sound you get with a disconnected number. I'd never thought much of it before. I hear it now and it's like I can't breathe. But I don't want to hang up…"

"You know what? You should move in with me for a while. I could use the company. You could use the company. You could help me pick out some better wine."

Kiki smiled. It would be nice. To not be alone. To feel a little safer.

Monday Morning

The ringing woke Clay. The green glow of the alarm clock read 3:07. He clicked on the bedside lamp. His first hazy thoughts focused on the idea that Eva had been hurt and someone was calling from the hospital. He moved as quickly as his exhausted, half-asleep body allowed. Before going to bed, he had doubled the dose of his sleeping medication; it made him feel drunk. It was only when he stood up that he realized he was naked; the clothes he had worn to bed were balled up in the far corner of the bedroom. The clothes looked wet. There were spots of mud on the carpet. Or was it blood?

He tried not to think, to remember, pushing back against the memories from his latest nighttime wandering; the developing images formed an uncomfortable blending of dream and reality.

Moving from the bedroom to the living room, Clay reached the phone on the fourth or fifth ring. "Hello?" His voice sounded hard and far away.

"I need you to see something." The detective's baritone voice rattled through the receiver with a jarring abruptness.

"Now?" Clay demanded after adjusting to the shock of hearing the detective's voice. "It's three o'clock in the morning. What in the hell is that important?"

"Grab a pen and write this address down. I'm telling you, you're going to want to see this."

Clay turned on a light, found a pen, and scribbled down the address on the palm of his hand.

"You need to hurry. Forensics is on its way."

"Forensics? What are you dragging me into?"

"You're wasting time. Just get your ass over here."

After hanging up the phone, Clay looked again at the address. It was in the Central District. Not far from the Nichols' house. The curiosity of a moment ago had morphed into an uncomfortable surge of anxiety. He had a vague idea of what the detective would show him, and part of him wished he could crawl back into bed, pull the covers up, and pretend the phone had never rung. Not that he would sleep. He would only lie there and obsess about the detective's discovery; why his clothes were wet and wadded up in the corner; what he had done during his wandering around.

Looking down, he saw that both of his hands were red, as if scrubbed raw to remove a stain.

The drive through the empty streets intensified the anxiety. He knew what was coming. There would be a body. That was obvious. The deeper question centered on whose body he would encounter. Would he recognize it? It seemed unlikely, but something nagged at him. Like a warning. As if what he expected was not what he would get.

And as the pale streetlights flickered past, something about the gray night felt familiar. The lack of rain. The way the clouds sat close overhead like a weight bearing down on the city. He had driven this set of streets hundreds of times. But that was not what made him want to stop and turn around. It was more about the fleeting mood and color filling the area that made him wonder if he had come this way while sleepwalking.

It took ten minutes to reach the address. As he pulled up, somewhat to his dismay, there were no blue and red flashing police lights. In fact, there were no police anywhere. The address the detective had given was nothing more than a dark, abandoned-looking house. Once he stepped out of the car, he spotted the detective walking up the street towards him.

"We're back this way," he said with a wave of his hand.

"Where is everyone?" Clay asked after a quick jog to catch up to the detective. "By the tone of your voice I figured there'd be a battalion of police cars here."

"I haven't called this in yet. I was waiting for you."

Clay slowed and nearly stopped. "Why?"

The detective glanced back. "I'll explain when we get there. Come on!"

About half a block up, the detective took a left and started down a wastewater gulley filled with tall, reedy grasses. Clay hesitated. Something felt off about this. Like a trap. Why else would he wait to call in a dead body? The reeds surrounding the narrow trail quickly swallowed up the detective. A sour mix of emotions roiled away in Clay's stomach. He considered turning back but, instead, stepped off the sidewalk and into the marshy overgrowth. The shorter shoots of grass popped and snapped beneath his feet. The fetid smell of stagnant water scented the air. And despite the cool temperature, Clay felt himself sweating.

Not long after entering the tall reeds, he lost sight of the detective and could no longer hear any movement ahead of him. "Where are you?"

"Follow the trail. I'm just a few yards farther."

In the faint glow of a nearby streetlight Clay finally reached a small clearing where he could see the outline of the detective. The detective pointed down at something in the shallow swampy water filling the base of the gully. A body. Clay lost his balance and had to grab the detective's arm as his feet sank into the mud. The large figure lay face up, the head not far from where Clay stood. Even in the dim light, the man's black visage was visibly bloodied and swollen. It was difficult to put a definite age to the disfigured face, but he looked young. The man was tall, maybe six foot four, and must have weighed close to 300 pounds. The eyes were open. Clay, still clutching the detective's jacket, tried to steady himself in the thick mud. His mouth had gone dry, and his stomach had tightened.

"What am I looking at?"

"You recognize him?" the detective asked.

Clay managed to pull his eyes away from the body to look at the detective. "Recognize him? No. Why the hell would I recognize him?"

The detective seemed to study Clay for a moment before answering. "I think this is our missing witness."

"Witness to what?"

"The double homicide. I'm guessing this is the man who watched the shooting of the Nichols brothers. You do remember me explaining that to you, about the fourth person in the house at the time of the shooting?"

"I remember," Clay said with a nod, his breath coming in short, hard gasps as if he had just finished running. His attention returned to the body. "How did you find him?"

"I put him here."

"What!"

The detective nearly fell over laughing. "A joke. Relax. I got a tip from a contact of mine."

"What makes you think this guy was at the house?"

"If you had been listening, and I'm starting to think you weren't, you would remember me explaining that whoever moved that couch was a big man. Also, this guy was shot in the head with a high-caliber handgun, which matches the way the brothers were shot. And I'll bet a year's salary that once the ballistics are done on this guy's head wound it will match the weapon used to kill the two brothers."

Clay cautiously leaned over, his hands resting on his knees for balance. The man had not been killed here. Even he could see that. The surrounding grass looked untouched except for the path leading down to the body.

"Why would they drag him here?"

"Not sure."

Clay straightened up. "Why are you showing me this? You could have waited until I got into work and told me over the phone. Or even taken pictures and shown those to me." Clay's left foot made a sucking sound as he pulled it out of the muck. His head ached, and a heavy exhaustion weighed on his shoulders, a reminder that he had not slept but an hour or two.

"I wanted to see your reaction."

The dead man's face reflected a waxy sheen in the charcoal-gray light. "And did I give the reaction you expected?"

"I'm a little disappointed. I'd hoped for more facial discoloration, perhaps a bout of vomiting."

Clay looked in the direction of the detective. The comment's sarcasm also held an undercurrent of irritation. "Why did you bring me here?" The light was at the detective's back, keeping his face in shadow.

"Well," the detective started, scratching at his head, "while I was out doing rounds earlier tonight, you wouldn't believe who I saw not a mile from here?"

Clay gave an indifferent shrug even as he felt himself tense up. "Who did you see?"

The detective turned his head slightly. Clay could see his face now. His eyes stared at him as if looking for something hidden.

"You. I saw you."

"Me?" Instead of expressing surprise, though, Clay's voice sounded resigned. He glanced at the body and then to his mud-covered shoes. The initial rush of seeing the dead man had shifted to something more like stressed uneasiness.

"I've seen a lot of crazy shit doing this job. But seeing you at two in the morning about sent me to the hospital. And you looked like you just got out of bed. You were dressed in sweats, and I'm not even sure you had shoes on," the detective said. "I passed you going the opposite direction, but by the time I turned around you were gone."

"How can you be so certain it was me?"

"I know white people look a lot alike, but it was you," the detective said with a dry, frustrated-sounding laugh. "And if that wasn't odd enough, this little encounter happened right before I got the call about the body."

"It's possible."

"Possible. What does that mean?"

Clay closed his eyes, a roiling upset growing in his abdomen. He did not want to have this conversation. He tried to formulate an avenue of lies that would get him out of this. But words were hard right then. And the energy needed for the deceit went in other directions. "It could have been me."

"Could have been you! Were you up here or not?"

"I'm not sure." The three-word statement made an effortless mix of truth and lies.

"How could you not know?"

"I sleepwalk sometimes."

"Wait! Did you say you sleepwalk?"

"I'm just telling you why you might have seen me, and why I don't remember being up here earlier."

"You're crazier than I thought, telling me you leave your apartment without shoes and wander around the city asleep. Do you really expect me to believe that?" Anger had entered the detective's voice. "Because if I didn't know better, I might think you're trying to insult my intelligence."

"When you woke me up, my hair was damp and my clothes were balled up in the corner soaking wet," Clay responded. He tried to keep his voice even and calm. "I

76

might have been up here. I just don't know where I went or how long I was out."

The eastern sky had grown visible with the first hint of morning light.

"Is that even a real thing? To sleepwalk in the middle of a busy city, for Christ's sake!"

Clay offered another noncommittal shrug. "I've done it since I was little." His eyes stared at the unmoving mass stretched out in front of him. So still. Almost unreal. It was hard to believe the man had been alive not that long ago. The stagnant, marshy smell of the water, the exhaustion, the cold air, all of it made his head throb. "You're welcome to talk to my doctor if you don't believe me. Better yet, talk to my mom. She'll happily tell you a bunch of horror stories of my midnight wanderings."

"Of all the crazy shit I've ever heard, this goes towards the top. So, I guess you don't remember dragging the body here, then?"

Clay gave a grunt-like laugh. The tone of the detective's voice made it difficult to tell if he was kidding or not. "I doubt I could even lift this guy's legs, let alone drag him anywhere." Clay needed to leave. That feeling of anxious unease grew. He wanted to get back home, go to bed, and pretend none of this had happened.

"I'll tell you what," the detective said with an impatient wave, "I don't like coincidences. I don't like the fact I see you near here right before I get a call about this body. You understand what I'm saying?"

"No, I don't understand," Clay responded with a spike of anger in his own voice. "If you think I have anything to do with this body, you're crazier than I am. I have no fucking idea how this guy ended up in this ditch. I don't even know who he is."

The detective appeared to study something near the body; or maybe he was trying to get his own anger under control. "We're done here. It's time for you to leave so I can call this in and get this process started. It's going to be a long goddamn morning."

"Do you have an ID for him?" Clay softened the tone of his voice. Despite the flash of anger, he needed to remain on good terms with the detective if he hoped to finish the crime statistics story.

"It's hard to tell with the damage to the head and face, but I'm pretty sure his name is Russell. He's a cousin of the two brothers."

"A cousin?"

"Yep. I've been trying to track him down, but no one had seen him in a couple of days." The detective's voice had a distracted quality to it as if he were thinking of something else.

"When I get into the newsroom later, should I call you or the communications department about this? I'll need to write up something."

"Call me. I should be back at my desk by ten."

"I appreciate you calling me on this. I know you didn't have to do that. And I apologize for snapping at you."

"I'll make you a deal – I won't make crazy accusations as long as I don't see you wandering around one of my crime scenes in the middle of the night. Fair enough?"

Clay nodded and looked back at the body. It felt as if he should do something, as if there were something that he could do for this man. After a couple of quiet moments, he turned and started up the uneven trail. It was going to be a struggle to get into work today. To do anything today.

Saturday

Before unlocking the apartment, Kiki gave several hard knocks on the door as if to warn anyone lurking inside. Melanie stood next to her. She didn't ask why Kiki had knocked. She seemed to understand.

"Do you want me to go first?" Melanie asked.

"No, I'm fine." Kiki took out her keys and opened the door.

Melanie had tried to make her feel safe, telling her she had nothing to fear. It didn't feel that way, though. Safe was the last word Kiki would have used to describe how she felt.

Once inside the apartment, Kiki turned on each light she passed even though it was two in the afternoon and a rare burst of winter sunshine poured in through the windows. Kiki stopped as she reached the entrance to the bedroom. She flipped on the light. The closed blinds created a twilight aspect to the room. She went to the closet and pushed clothes out of the way to expose anything hidden; she looked under the bed; she pulled out each drawer of the dresser. Everything appeared untouched. Normal. Just as she had left it on Friday. Like nothing had happened. But neither the search nor the pronouncement that things looked all right helped to calm her mood.

"You don't have to do this yet," Melanie said, putting an arm across Kiki's shoulder. "You can stay at my place as long as you want."

Kiki had awoken that morning disoriented. It had taken a few moments to recall where she had spent the night. She didn't like how it felt being away from home. It made her feel lost, weak, afraid.

"I need to come back sometime," Kiki said. "I can't imagine it will get any easier. Besides, the building manager said he would replace the lock today."

"I wish I could stay longer. My shift ends at nine. Call me if there are any problems. You have a key to my apartment. Just come over if you need to. Okay?"

"Thank you."

"Promise you'll come over if anything happens or you don't feel safe?"

"Yes."

"I'll call you when I get home."

After letting Melanie out, Kiki pushed the couch against the door and set it up with sheets and a blanket with the idea of sleeping there for the night. She felt uncertain about what to do next. Afraid to move from the couch, she lay down, her eyes moving back and forth, scanning the room for the slightest movement.

It had never occurred to her how many noises an old apartment building made, or the unending racket tenants created with their loud voices and slamming doors. She tried to relax and reassure herself that everything would be fine. This had been home for five years. She didn't need to be afraid. But even as she thought this, the fear that kept her on edge continued to grow.

Needing to do something, Kiki got up and went to the cedar table and Nana's mass of research material. She took a loose set of photocopies from the top of one of the piles: a pioneer journal. Kiki's eyes stared at the words on the sheet in front of her. Seeing, but not seeing. Her grandmother had collected so much stuff it was impossible to separate the important from the garbage. The first page of the diary had the name Hattie written at the top.

It was dark when we reached Mt. Pleasant. Papa has spent the last hour yelling at Ma about being behind schedule because Abby and me take too long to get going in the morning. Abby cries from all the yelling. I try to quiet her since her crying only makes Papa angrier.

There wasn't much to identify the young author except that she had started the journal shortly after her thirteenth birthday. The journal centered on her family's journey in 1867 from Illinois to the Washington Territory. The family consisted of Hattie's mom, dad, and little sister, Abby. Much of the account had a travel log tone to it as Hattie described the terrain and challenges of moving through great swaths of wilderness on the way west.

We've entered Indian Territory. The men of the wagon train voted Papa as one of the group leaders tonight because of his military service. It was a good night. Papa was happy because of the men's trust in him. Abby and me pretended to be soldiers in his new army, marching around the campfire and saluting him at every pass. Both Ma and he laughed a great deal at that.

The father, Kiki soon realized, had a violent temper he primarily directed at his wife and children. Hattie blamed this viciousness on her father's service in the Union Army during the Civil War. The father's unpredictable violence made sections of the diary difficult to read.

In other parts, the narrative got lost in the minutiae of the wagon train to the point where Kiki would turn the page and could not recall what she had just read. About three-quarters the way through, however, Hattie's journal entries focused on her mother's deteriorating health. Over the course of several days, Hattie described her mother suffering from a high fever and frequent stops along the trail because of diarrhea and vomiting. Cholera, Kiki thought. She had never seen it at the hospital, but she knew the symptoms; and she knew this was not going to end well unless Hattie's mother received treatment for severe dehydration. Without help, her mother's blood pressure would drop, and catastrophic renal failure would soon follow. The subsequent entries grew more and more despondent, culminating on July 5:

> *Woke to a terrible silence this morning. Fell asleep last night listening to Mama's labored breathing. But this morning I couldn't hear anything. No wind. Not even the movement of the oxen or horses. When I got up I found Mama's blanket empty. Couldn't see much as it was just before dawn. But I could hear digging not far away.*

Looking up from the journal, Kiki realized she had been reading for more than two hours. Her eyes hurt. She got up from the table and wandered over to the three rectangular windows looking out at the street below. She wondered if she should look for a new place to live, somewhere she could feel safe; the thought of moving, though, left its own kind of tired emptiness. She loved the neighborhood. The view from her windows. The quick commute to work. In the distance, a small break in the overcast sky near downtown sent a shock of color across the drab landscape.

> *I spotted Pa working in the middle of the wagon trail. Graves, we'd been told, needed to be in the trail to keep the wolves and Indians from digging them up. I kept quiet as I moved closer. Mama lay not far from the trail. I held her hand. No warmth to Mama's skin. Her eyes were closed. Her skin and muscles felt like*

pieces of tired earth. When Pa finished digging, he
pushed me away from Mama and yelled at me to get
back to the wagon. I wouldn't go. So he dragged me
as I cried and screamed. He must have hit me at some
point because I found myself in the dirt. I returned to
where Mama was and watched him wrap her in a
quilt and set her body into the shallow pit. I watched
him cover the body with dirt. No marker. Just a small
mound of dirt the wagons will drive over and flatten
out.

Kiki looked at the couch still wedged against the
door. She knew that once she left the apartment there
would be no way to know if someone had entered or not.
No way to know if someone waited for her to return. The
building manager had come and changed the lock, but
that didn't make her feel any better. The man had broken
in so easily before. A new lock didn't seem much of a
deterrent.

Traveling through high desert now. After making
supper I took a walk to get away from Pa and Abby
and found a small stream not far and followed it until
I could no longer hear the rumblings of the camp.
Only the sound of the water. Wished it could always
be like this. So much noise and rocking when riding
in the wagon. Even when stopped I still hear the loud
creaking and feel all that movement.

Leaving the window, she went to the kitchen and
poured a cup of coffee. When she reached for the sugar
bowl, the smooth glazed surface slipped from her grasp
and sent the container off the counter and shattering
against the yellow and white paisley-patterned kitchen
floor. Shards of gray pottery exploded in all directions. A
sick, dizzy feeling filled Kiki's head. The bowl was
nothing fancy. Just a small clay pot with a lid. But it had

been a gift from Nana. Kiki's hands shook as she knelt to pick up the larger fragments and drop them into the nearby trashcan. So many pieces. Too many. She leaned back and slumped to the floor, resting against a kitchen cabinet. Blood dripped from a cut on her hand. The granulated sugar and pottery chips spread across the length of the kitchen and extended into the dining room area. Pieces had scattered in all directions. No longer whole. A million fragments she would never put back together.

> *We reached the river at Fish Falls. We've traveled most of the last two days without fresh water or any foraging for the animals. Once we leave here, there will be more waterless days ahead as we'll travel above the river canyon. Abby barely talks. I guess I've grown quiet too. Pa don't care much as his attention is with the running of the wagon train.*

It took a while before Kiki got up from the floor. She wasn't sure how long. The light outside had grown grayer; but that could have been from a heavier cloud cover as much as a later time in the day. She returned to the table and stared at the journal. Words. Her eyes moved from the journal to the mess still spread across the kitchen floor, and then back to the journal.

> *Set up camp at Three Island Crossing. I'm tired. At times it's like I sleep with my eyes open while riding along in the wagon I get so lost in my thoughts. Pa plans to cross in the morning even though the river is running high. Watched several wagons cross today. River bottom is uneven. One horse nearly disappeared beneath the water after moments before being completely dry.*

The wooden, ladder-back chair creaked as Kiki sat up and tried to focus. She read the next journal entry several times, going over each word as if it described something unbelievable. The words were written in a blocky, middle-school cursive. The lines connecting the letters looked slightly off, a little more ragged than the previous journal entries. Kiki leaned forward and rubbed her temples, thinking of the high desert's rainless heat and the dusty, dry earth. At some point, she stood and went into the kitchen to sweep up the sugar and scattered pottery shards; the events described in the journal served as a harsh reminder of her own painful losses.

Abby's body surfaced a mile down river. The men buried her on the north side of Three Island above the flood line. Only remember a little of what happened. I remember Abby and me sitting next to Pa on the wagon seat. I was in the middle and Abby was on the outside. There was a slow wariness as we entered the water. Pa kept careful track to follow the wagon ahead. It wasn't long after we reached the deepest section of river that I heard shouting and then felt something large hit the wagon and pitch it sideways and into the water. I hit the water before I could take a breath. Something landed on top of me. Might have been Abby. We got tangled for a few seconds and then separated and I tumbled along the river bottom, the water holding me under and running me downstream until I got snarled in a jumble of low-hanging willow branches and managed to get my head above water.

Only a couple of pages remained. Kiki remembered her trip with Nana through Southern Idaho when she was twelve. Pale-blue sagebrush peppered the rugged volcanic terrain, the barren Owyhee Mountains to the south and the giant sky overhead.

Upriver Pa struggled to unhitch the oxen as the river rushed around the wagon and threatened to take the whole mess to the sea. I looked for Abby. There were men wading into the water. I tried to go back into the main flow of the river to look for her but someone picked me up and set me on the bank. I sit not far from the fresh dug earth of Abby's grave. No grave marker for her. Just like Mama. Don't want to draw attention to the dead. Pa tells me we leave in the morning.

Someone had scribbled an address at the bottom of the last page. A Seattle address located in the Pioneer Square area. The handwriting looked similar to that of the journal entries, suggesting Hattie had written it. The date below the address put it prior to the 1889 fire that destroyed much of Seattle's downtown. Part of that burnt-out city, Kiki knew, remained buried beneath the present-day brick buildings.

Kiki started to look through the pile of books stacked across the table for a pre-1889 street map. Despite a deep anxiety about going outside, she needed fresh air, needed to separate herself from the oppressive space of the apartment that had begun to weigh on her like a prison cell.

3:40 p.m.

The low-angled sun offered scant comfort against the soggy winter chill. Kiki stood on the sidewalk, eyes closed, face turned in the direction of a sliver of sunlight squeezed between the surrounding buildings. Pioneer Square was all but deserted. A nearby delivery truck accelerated, bringing with it the stink of diesel exhaust and the strained wheeze of overburdened suspension springs.

As the daylight dimmed, Kiki returned to the book that contained a map of Seattle from 1885. She oriented it to the current street layout and tried to visualize the wooden city that had burned to the ground in 1889. In pencil, she had put an X next to where the address at the end of the journal was most likely located. It would be buried now, the area's current brick buildings serving as the gravestones for that blackened city. It felt strange being there with almost no one else around. Unlike most of the city, something close to history hovered in the air around Pioneer Square.

She took a deep breath, her head filling with the smells of Puget Sound: a mixture of creosote, organic decay, and saltwater. Her thoughts calmed. The periodic cries of seagulls wove into the low hum of city sounds. The 1889 fire started around noon on June 6. It had been an unusually dry spring, and with most of the buildings made of rough-hewn timber, the fire caught on quickly fanned by strong winds. The flames spread across a 120-

acre swath of downtown in a matter of hours. The fire, in due course, reached nearby storage bunkers that contained some 300 tons of coal. The coal burned for days, producing a thick layer of black smoke that smothered the city during the day and created a hellish crimson glow at night. The post-fire photographs she had seen showed an apocalyptic landscape of blackened skeletal forms.

Kiki crossed to the east side of the street. In the near distance loomed the Kingdome. The squat concrete mushroom fit in well with the rest of the ugly iron railroad tracks and large port cranes that scarred the waterfront. The burning coalbunkers, she thought, would have found a suitable home in this hard, unnatural landscape.

At the corner of Washington Street and First Avenue, the odor of stale beer from the nearby bars replaced the sea-smells. But it wasn't just the smells that had changed. Kiki looked around. The sun was in the middle of another brief clearing. She felt watched, even though Pioneer Square remained mostly empty. She scanned the nearby cars: all unoccupied. There was a small group of homeless men congregating at Occidental Square Park. Several tourists walked the sidewalks. Shading her eyes, she searched the surrounding buildings, attempting to see past the glare in the windows of the shops and upper-floor apartments. Nothing. The feeling, however, persisted as she started to walk again.

If the details on the map were correct, the address had to be close. But it was hard to tell. The current street configuration didn't match up with the pre-fire layout. She closed the book and continued up First Avenue. Back in high school, her Northwest history class had taken the Pioneer Square underground tour. She tried to remember something of that subterranean geography, the alignment of the streets, anything. But there were only vague memories of dusty-gray light, unstable-looking wooden and brick supports, and the smell of mildew. The tour guide had been more interested in telling ghost stories than relating any actual history about the underground ruins. Maybe it was the memory of those stories that sent a chill across her skin, as if there was something to fear down here. The thought made her laugh; she already had more phantoms haunting her than she could handle.

Kiki slowed and then stopped halfway down the block. Movement from a second-story window on the other side of the street caught her attention. The glare on the glass made it difficult to see in, but Kiki thought she saw a figure. A woman. Kiki crossed First Avenue. A luminescent moss grew in patches across the weathered red brick of the building's façade. As she approached, the female figure faded and reappeared with the changing direction of the light.

The building's street-level retail space sat empty. A sun-faded "For Lease" sign was propped up against the dusty window. Brittle, brown leaves piled against the barred door that led to the upper floors. The tags next to the apartment buzzers were either empty or too faded to read. Kiki looked back up at the second-story window. Just the reflection of the surrounding trees and buildings now. Maybe the woman had walked away. It certainly seemed possible. Everything felt possible. Like a fever-induced hallucination.

The wind blew and scratched the dried leaves against the sidewalk, a sound not unlike fingernails on a chalkboard.

Up the street, the white cross atop of the Union Gospel Mission building glimmered in the afternoon sun.

Kiki pressed each of the four apartment intercom buttons and waited. No response. She opened the book and looked at the map. The address from the journal could have been around this spot. On the opposing page from the map, she read a section covering the 1889 fire. The book quoted a woman who had seen the fire shortly after it started: *The flames moved as if alive,* the passage read, *traveling from one building to the next with a God-like purposefulness.*

Above, the upper-story windows remained empty. The wooden window frames looked rotted out from too many gray Seattle winters. She pressed the buzzers again and then cupped her hands and leaned against the iron bars protecting the glass door. Dust and random pieces of trash covered the wooden stairs leading to the upper floors. A noise close to laughter escaped Kiki's lips. Not an amused laugh. The sound carried a more confused and melancholy tone as she wondered what she was doing down her anyway. She felt tired. Exhausted. She needed to sleep but didn't want to return to her apartment. Wasn't sure if she ever wanted to go back. Melanie wouldn't return from work until later in the evening.

Stepping away from the door, she copied down the barely legible phone number written on the "For Lease" sign. There was something about this place. Something familiar. But maybe that came from the need for additional distractions, a wished-for connection. Whatever the reason, it didn't really matter. Either way. She would call the number later and ask if it was possible to have a look inside the building.

7:10 p.m.

The microwave dinged. Clay got up from the couch, went into the kitchen, and removed a steaming bag of teriyaki beef and an equally searing bag of rice. He poured the contents of both into a bowl and returned to the living room. The salty, processed food was skin-blistering hot. A generic car commercial played on the television. He muted the sound with the plan to keep it off until the Sonics game started. The disjointed anger and frustration from the previous day's encounter with the detective continued to roil away in the background despite his best efforts to push it aside. His attention focused on the car commercial's quick-cut images of speed and sex and wealth and a world where the only concerns centered on winding roads and beloved friends. He would like that. To live in a world like that, an impossible-to-exist world.

The flickering light from the TV along with the weak glow of the small table lamp did little to push back the darkness that weighed down the rest of the apartment, making the nearly windowless space shrink even more, intensifying the tomb-like oppressiveness. At times, it felt like the building's upper floors were slowly pushing down on him, suffocating him. When he came out to see the apartment for the first time, the advertisement had called it a daylight basement; the only light that reached these depths, however, was the electric kind. The apartment had ten-foot-high ceilings, which made the space feel bigger; but, in return, it only had two narrow, rectangular windows perched some eight feet from the floor with views of a below-level window well. The living room and kitchen shared the same open space. As for the closet-like bedroom, there were no windows at all. The apartment, on a good day, felt mildly claustrophobic. He had considered moving, but the rent was cheap and the location, at the foot of Queen Anne, was convenient to everything.

Clay sat back and tried to settle into a more comfortable position on the old couch. The worn piece of mid-century-modern furniture had been his grandparents'. And, in a way, that was nice. But he kept it because he had gotten it free and he didn't see a good reason to buy a new one. For him, the gold geometric patterns sewn across the white fabric fell just short of ugly; and the memories the couch evoked ran from mildly pleasant to extremely disagreeable. It came from a time when his mom and dad were still married, a time when the extended family – aunts, uncles, cousins – spent Christmas together at his grandparents'. The memories included the sound of tearing wrapping paper, the cousins putting on plays and running around chasing each other. But there were other parts, too, disagreeable parts, such as the heavy drinking and the loud and angry verbal altercations that invariably arose and threw off the already impossible fantasy of family love and affection.

Clay tested the steaming food but found it still too hot. He picked up the remote and turned the television sound back on, increasing the volume to drown out the internal clatter filling his head. With only a couple of minutes until tipoff, the commentators talked about the team matchups. Their words were simple, augmented by pictures and graphics. More than anything, Clay wanted to focus on that. To forget. To get away from the jumble of noises and images that filled the world around him and created an intense knot of tension across his shoulders, neck, and back. The chatter of voices, however, did little to alleviate any of the pressure. He took a bite from the teriyaki bowl. The salty-brown-sugar mixture burned his tongue and lips as his teeth ground away at the meat, rice, and vegetables.

The image on the television switched to a wide shot of the basketball court. The players gathered at the half-court circle. The referee tossed the ball into the air and the game began. Clay put his feet on the coffee table in a gesture meant to convey a state of calm relaxation. But his muscles tensed even more. He tried to ignore this. To stop thinking. To force his mind to be at ease.

1:18 a.m.

With the couch wedged back against the door, Kiki sat down and rested her head in her hands. She had searched the apartment. Nothing out of place. Everything where it should be. But that hadn't made any difference in how she felt. In the past, she used to look forward to this time of night after getting home from work when everything felt so quiet and peaceful. Not anymore. Every little sound set her on edge.

She stood and walked to the window. Even the rain, once a reliable source of comfort, did nothing to calm the near-constant pulse of anxiety. Her eyes followed the raindrops falling past the window on down to the sidewalk where the water collected in a series of slowly expanding puddles.

Exhaustion urged her to lie down and close her eyes. She had slept very little this past week. The lack of sleep made it hard to think. Even simple things, such as which bus to take to work, had required considerable effort.

One welcome surprise since getting home was a message on her answering machine from the owner of the Pioneer Square building. On Monday, Kiki had called the number from the "For Lease" sign, but it had connected her with a real estate broker. The man she talked to knew nothing about the history of the building; he took Kiki's phone number and said he would forward it to the building's owner. She had assumed that would mark the end of the inquiry. Instead, the owner had called and said she would be happy to answer any questions about the building's history. The woman had left a phone number and recommended calling in the afternoon. Kiki wished she could call now and have somewhere to focus her thoughts.

What would she ask, though? Had a woman named Hattie once lived in the burned-out ruins buried beneath the building? Or, perhaps, she could ask who the phantom figure in the window was? Either question, Kiki guessed, would quickly end the conversation, as the owner would mark her for crazy. Maybe if she kept the inquiry centered on the history of the building and what the owner knew about any of the building's occupants, she might get some of her questions answered.

Movement down on the sidewalk drew Kiki's attention. Across the street. At first, she thought it had been the wind. But when she cupped her hands to eliminate the glare from the apartment lights, she spotted a figure standing next to the leafless maple tree across the way, just beyond the glow of the nearby streetlight. She left the window and turned off the lights. With it dark, she watched as the person knelt and moved something on the sidewalk.

Kiki located her binoculars on the end table next to where the couch used to be. After a bit of adjusting, she brought the figure into focus. The man was standing now. He wore a hooded sweatshirt that hid his face. He seemed to point at something, as if he knew she was watching him. Kiki's hands shook. She tried to focus on the sidewalk. The shaking intensified the closer she zoomed in. He had put the rocks in a pattern. Letters, maybe. But with the rain and her inability to keep the binoculars steady, it was impossible to get a clear image of what she was looking at. When she returned to the figure, he appeared to stare up at her. She stumbled away from the window, nearly falling over the coffee table as she tried to regain her balance. Fear cleared her sleep-addled mind, sweeping away the exhaustion.

She tentatively returned to the window. The upper branches of the maple tree gave way to the man's hooded head and then the sidewalk. He started to walk away. Heading south. Without thinking, Kiki tossed the binoculars onto a chair, shoved the couch from the door, and rushed out of the apartment with no clear idea of what she was doing other than a vague notion to confront this person. Anger and fear had subverted caution. She should call the police. The thought repeated itself as she ran down the four flights of stairs, her feet skipping two stairs at a time even as she warned herself to stop. She quickly reached the lobby, burst out of the apartment building entrance, and turned south. But once outside, she found herself alone. The street ahead of her was empty. She slowed, uncertain, and jogged to the next cross street. Nothing. She looked back in the other direction: nothing but vacant sidewalk.

She had a difficult time breathing; she continued for another block. Nothing. Turning around, Kiki crossed the street and went to where the man had been standing near the maple tree. Just outside the circle of the streetlight, she found the rocks arranged to form the word STOP. Her chest hurt as she struggled to calm her breath. She scanned the surrounding area, half expecting to see the man sprinting towards her ready to hack her to pieces. But the street and sidewalk remained deserted. The city, except for the rhythm of the rain, stayed still and quiet. She didn't, couldn't, believe any of this was intended for her. That would have been crazy. Like seeing a ghost in an empty building. None of it to be trusted.

It wasn't long before the rain soaked her black hair and her green cotton hospital scrubs. The rain weighed everything down. Everything but her thoughts. Her thoughts held no weight at all. Each unmoored feeling, idea, or notion flitted around her like ashes scattering in the wind.

9:51 a.m.

Clay sat at the kitchen table. Same place he had sat for the past couple of hours. He was late for work. His wet clothes lay crumpled near the front door. He did not feel rested. It did not feel like he had slept at all. He tried not to care. About any of it. Ignoring as best he could the terrible mental pressure building inside of him.

The sound of the phone came from far away, ringing several times before he pushed himself up to answer it.

"Are you're coming in?" Melissa's voice snapped. She sounded her usual unpleasant self.

"I'm heading out the door now."

"Don't come to the newsroom. I need you to head over to Portage Bay. The police pulled a body from the water. Go there first and see what you can find out."

Clay took a seat on the couch, the fingers of his right hand spread out along the armrest. He was not sure he had the energy to leave the apartment. "A body?"

"Yes, Clay, a body," Melissa spat. "A dead body. Can you do this or not?"

What he wanted to tell Melissa was he that felt sick and was not going to make it in today. That was what he wanted to say. But those weren't the words that left his mouth. "What's the address?"

Melissa read off some numbers and a street name. "And when you're done there come straight to the newsroom so I can figure out how we're going to play this in tomorrow's paper."

For a moment, Clay considered telling her he did not want to do it; he did not want to do anything. But the moment passed. "All right. I'll see you in an hour or so."

"No detours, Clay."

He hung up but remained sitting on the couch. The idea of covering a murder and then writing a story about it felt like too much. He would have to talk to people at the crime scene; once he returned to the newsroom, there would be phone calls to make; and then he would have to write the story itself. It was too much, he thought. More than he could handle right now.

In the bathroom, Clay stripped off his damp underwear, turned on the shower, and stepped in. He had only intended to rinse off the sweat and dirt, but the warmth and calming rhythm of the water made it hard to leave. The delay left him in a rush to get dressed and out the door, forgetting to eat breakfast or shave the two days' growth of facial hair.

The Portage Bay address sat in the middle of a stretch of waterfront that consisted of houseboats, boat moorings, and industrial shipyards. It was not a place known for dredging up bodies. Clay picked up the piece of paper on the passenger seat to see the first couple of numbers of the address. Blue filled the sky overhead. Beautiful and unexpected. To the east, a bank of clouds gathered, promising an eventual end to this rare break in the winter gray.

The address proved easy to find as dozens of police cars and television news trucks concentrated around one of the bay's mooring docks. The crackle of a police radio and the low hum of truck generators echoed off the narrow stretch of water. As he approached the yellow police line, Clay spotted one of the newspaper's photographers standing on the roof of a car trying to get a better angle on the police boats in the distance.

"How things look, Jon?"

The photographer glanced in Clay's direction and then returned to looking through his camera. "What's up, Clay?"

"Any word on what they found?"

"Not much. I got here after they pulled the body from the water. Right now, there's a bunch of divers bobbing around. And as far as I can tell, they haven't pulled anything else from the bay."

"Have you heard anything about the body? Male? Female?"

"Nothing. And I don't have much in the way of usable art for the article. Just some images of police standing on a dock, police boats, and some unidentifiable dark spots in the water."

"Thanks."

Clay continued in the direction of the police line. If he was lucky, he might spot someone from the police department he knew and get more information that way. Taking his notebook out, he wrote down some of the details of the scene, gradually moving over to where the other reporters were gathered. He asked if they had heard anything. No one, of course, gave much away.

It took a few more minutes of wandering around before he located a detective he knew. "Detective Phillips," he shouted and walked along the line to get closer to where the man stood. The detective, not Clay's first choice, rarely gave any useful information, but he needed to start somewhere to narrow in on what was happening.

"My boy Clark," the detective said with a sarcastic curtness. "What can we do for you?"

Clay gave an exaggerated laugh at the detective's referring to him by Superman's alias. "I hear you found a body?" Clay said, his voice pitched with an affected cheerfulness.

"Well, way to go, Clark. Who says reporters don't know their mouth from their ass?"

Clay smiled and then waited a moment to see if Detective Phillips would volunteer any information. But nothing else followed. "Can you give me any details?"

"Nope," the detective said with a straight face. "Nothing worth sharing at this point."

"Man? Woman?"

"A man."

"Have you identified –"

"That's all, Clark. You can wait with the rest of the vultures for the press release." At that, Detective Phillips walked off in the direction of the water.

"Clay!"

The sound of a familiar voice issued from behind him. He turned and saw Detective Carpenter approaching from the direction of the road.

"Beautiful day," the detective said with a grin.

"Do you ever sleep?" Clay asked. His voice retained its artificial cheerfulness from talking with Detective Phillips.

"Only when I can no longer stay awake," the detective responded. He then ducked under the crime-scene tape and motioned for Clay to follow. "What about you? You look like you could use a little more rest. Or is that corpse-like pallor part of the new grunge style?"

Clay ignored the comment. "You know anything about what they found?"

The detective started to walk in the direction of the water. "Can't tell you much. Male. Sounds like he hasn't been in the water all that long, probably only a day or two."

"Do they know who he is?" Clay asked. He had to quicken his pace to keep up with the detective.

"Not sure. Just got here."

101

"Cause of death?"

"I just got here, Clay," the detective repeated with a stern look. "Let's see what we can find out."

In the distance, the head of a diver popped up from the dark water and made a series of hand signals to a nearby police boat.

The detective stopped as he reached the coroner's van parked in front of a gated chain-link fence. "Dave, you mind if I pull him out?" The detective directed his question to an overweight man wearing a stained and ill-fitting white lab coat. "My friend here thinks he might know the deceased."

"What?" Clay asked with a clipped laugh.

"Help yourself," the man answered and spat in the gravel next to the van. "It's on you if he touches it or fucks up anything."

The detective responded with a noncommittal grunt.

Clay glanced back. The van stood about thirty yards from the police line. "I might know who this is?" he asked the detective in a low whisper.

The detective ignored the question, opened the two white van doors, and rolled out the coroner's containment gurney. The grind of the trays metal wheels against the steel rails sent a piercing ring through the morning air.

Another body, Clay thought, anxiety digging at his nerves. He didn't want to see any more of the dead. Not now. Not with the mix of exhaustion and anxiety that stressed his head and body. The detective brought the gurney halfway out. The van's rooftop refrigeration unit hummed away while the scent of decay mixed with the acidic smell of antiseptic bleach, creating a queasy cloud of odors that worked disagreeably with Clay's empty stomach.

"You're not going to see much looking at your shoes," the detective said. He then unbuckled the top restraint and drew down the thick zipper of the black body bag.

102

Clay shifted his eyes to the detective's hand, watching it pull the zipper along its silver tracks until it stopped halfway down. The detective spread open the bag. The man was nude, his face badly swollen. The brown, bloodshot eyes stared up at the graying sky, and the black skin carried a waxy, candle-like appearance. A quarter-sized wound marked the spot where the man had been shot in the forehead. Clay's equilibrium slipped. The smell, maybe. Or the lack of sleep and food. He felt sick; his hand gripped the gurney for balance. He saw something familiar in the man's face: how it resembled the one in the drainage ditch, the bruising and swelling. And as Clay struggled to maintain composure, the vertigo accelerated, and a rush of vinegary bile filled his mouth, his reflexes barely quick enough to turn his head to avoid vomiting on the body itself.

"What the fuck!" the man in the lab coat shouted with a quick jerk back, nearly falling over in his haste to get out of the way.

Clay doubled over. A second muscle contraction of nausea took hold and what little stomach contents remained spat from his mouth. The detective patted Clay's back and said something about meatloaf.

The coroner's assistant, meanwhile, launched into a loud series of obscenities. "Christ, Carpenter! This is your goddamn fault. What in the fuck…"

With his hands on his knees and no longer looking at the body, Clay's stomach began to settle down.

"So what do you think, Dave, two days in the water?"

"What?" the fat man responded incredulously. "I don't fucking know. Jesus, he puked on my shoes! How am I going to get this off my shoes?"

"Do you recognize him, Clay?" the detective asked.

Clay glanced up at the detective. To his surprise, a pained express twisted the detective's face.

"Maybe," he said in a weak voice, wiping his mouth with the sleeve of his shirt.

103

"He was with Redman on Friday," the detective stated. "He was one of the boys in the alleyway."

Clay remembered now: a partly shadowed face near the edge of the group. He was the one Detective Carpenter had singled out for laughing after the detective had slapped Redman.

"A gunshot wound," the detective mumbled. He was leaning over the body and inspecting the dead man's hands. "Interesting."

"What is it?" Clay asked and spat into the gravel to try to remove the foul taste in his mouth. He remained slightly bent over, unwilling to stand up and see the body again.

"Look at this," the detective said with a poke at Clay's back. "Come on. Stand up, you're fine."

Clay straightened and tentatively looked in the direction of the body bag. He avoided the man's face and focused on the area the detective was pointing out.

The detective had put on latex gloves and was holding up one of the man's hands. "There are signs of a struggle," he said. "Look at the knuckles. Skin scraped clean off. Blood. Probably not just his own blood, either. This boy put up a fight. Whoever did this is nursing some of his own wounds. Any sign of water in the lungs, Dave?"

The man was attempting to clean off his shoes with a wad of paper towels. "You'll have to wait for the goddamn report. Will you look at my shoes! Jesus! I'm going to have to change these fucking things now."

"He's naked, too," the detective said and placed the arm back inside the bag. "Could have been taking a shower at the time of the attack. Could have been in bed. The killer beat him up pretty good. Look at all this bruising. Must have had some questions he wanted answered before he shot him."

Clay was looking towards the water. "Any chance this is connected to the two brothers who were killed?"

104

"Keep up the good police work, Dave. I don't believe any of those rumors about you and the farm animals."

The large-bellied man managed a laugh. "Keep an eye out for the cleaning bill I'm sending you!"

The detective began to walk towards the open gate that led to the dock. Clay, unsure of what to do, followed him.

"As far as a connection between this murder and the two brothers, who knows?" the detective said. "My gut tells me these are linked. But the ballistics from the gunshot wound will be the key. What I want to know, though, is whether our boy there will warrant more than a paragraph in the back of tomorrow's paper? Or is he not quite white enough? We could dump him back in the water and wait until the fish eat the meat from the bones."

"You're complaining to the wrong person. If you want this story to get better play, you need to give me something that connects this to those other murders," Clay said. The two men walked down the weatherworn dock, their footsteps creating a hollow, outsized echo.

"I'll see what I can do. Can't promise anything…" The detective's voice trailed off.

At the water's edge, moored houseboats occupied both sides of the dock, unmoving in the gentle waters of the bay.

"Any additional information on the deceased would also help. Like a name? Criminal background? Where he lives? The more I know, the better story I can present to my editor."

The detective, however, did not seem to hear him. He cupped his hands in front of his mouth and shouted at a figure at the end of the dock. "What's the word, Scott?"

The man, who wore the silver bar of a lieutenant, turned and grinned when he saw Detective Carpenter. "Legs! Spread the word!" he yelled back.

"Christ, Lieutenant, ladies are present," the detective said with a thumb pointing at Clay.

"My pardon, newspaper girl."

"Anything new?"

The man gave a quick glance in Clay's direction. "Maybe, but nothing I'd want to read about in the paper just yet. I take that back, we did find a rusted-out '82 Oldsmobile down in the muck of the bay. You interested?"

"Only if I can give it to my ex-wife as a birthday present," the detective said.

The lieutenant gave Clay another hard look. "If your friend will pardon us, I can get you caught up."

The detective motioned for Clay to head back up the dock. "I'll meet you back at the tape."

As Clay walked up the dock, he thought he heard the lieutenant say something about another body. But that was it. Within a couple of steps, he had moved out of hearing range. The clouds he had seen earlier had arrived, blanketing the sky in a dull metallic silver. The weather report predicted a light rain sometime in the afternoon. Since September, Seattle had seen a mere three full days of clear skies. It was now February.

Before exiting through the dock security gate, he scribbled down some of the visual details. He made a note about the high-end houseboats that mixed with a handful of run-down residences, several of which were listing and appeared on the verge of sinking. There was the hollow echo of the police radios that sounded across the choppy, dark green waters of the bay. And the body. He forced himself to write a brief description. The image hovered at the front of his mind: the bloodless gunshot wound, the pruned hands, chipped fingernails, and the swollen, deep blue coloring of the skin.

Clay reached the police tape and ducked under, standing now on the shoulder of the narrow residential road. He looked for the photographer, Jon, but no longer saw him or the car he had been standing on. That was all right. Jon had seen him and could corroborate Clay's presence at the crime scene, just in case there were any problems with Melissa. He should start thinking about getting back, though. Melissa would want an update. He made a half-hearted search for a payphone, but there was nothing around.

A bit of sunlight broke through the thickening clouds. Clay raised a hand to soften the glare. Against the light, his fingers appeared thin and frail, the skin becoming translucent to the point where the bones seemed almost visible. Like a ghost. As if he were losing his physical self.

A series of shouts drew his attention back to the water, words echoing incoherently through the air. Some twenty yards off the dock, a diver had a hand up, motioning to one of the nearby boats to come closer.

"...something here," a voice echoed.

The police radios began to crackle with activity and a boat from across the bay started back in the direction of the diver.

Not long after that, Detective Carpenter ambled up the dock. "Wouldn't mind having a house down here," he said, taking a moment to look towards the water.

"Is it another body?" Clay asked.

"Not sure. You okay? You look like you might get sick again."

Clay watched as several divers dropped into the water from a nearby police boat. "I'm fine," he said. That was not how he felt, though. He could not remember when he had last eaten; he wondered if that might be part of the problem. "How about you, are you all right? You didn't look all that well when you opened the bag."

"This whole thing has a bad feel to it," the detective said. "More than just a series of random drive-bys. The killer has something bigger in mind. On top of that, I put out some feelers earlier in the week to locate Redman and no one has seen him. I'm a little concerned I'll find his body next."

"What do you think is going on?"

The detective glanced back at the media trucks and the growing number of spectators. "Something drug related, I would guess. But anything's possible."

Voices and the sound of accelerating boat engines ricocheted across the water. "By the way, you've gotten your point across," Clay said.

"Have I now? And what point is that?"

"About the bodies. Showing me the bodies. You're trying to get to me. Right? Teach me a lesson about how hard and brutal a murder investigation can be. Maybe get me to do something embarrassing, like throwing up. And that's fine. Mission accomplished. But I get it now. You don't need to show me any more bodies. In fact, I'd prefer if you didn't show me any more."

"Okay. You're wrong. But okay," the detective said. There was a note of disappointment in his voice that surprised Clay. "What I wanted you to do, the reason I'm showing you the bodies, is to get you to see them like a clue, a piece within a larger puzzle. Dwelling on the humanity of the dead is a distraction. There's too much emotion in that. The key is to make the necessary connections between the dead, the crime scene, and the killer. To do that, you need to remove the emotion. You follow me?"

Clay gave a short nod.

"To be honest," the detective added, "these homicides are a little more challenging than most as far as keeping emotionally neutral. For one, I know many of these kids. And there's the fact these boys aren't much older than my daughters. Makes it tough. And trust me, this is far from over. I guarantee that."

Small jagged pieces of gravel lined the road's shoulder, interspersed with patches of exposed earth where cars had cleared the rocks away. Part of what the detective said felt true about why he was showing him the bodies. But only part. There was more to it. Like the

108

detective was testing him, looking for signs of guilt and weakness. Clay warned himself to be careful. To watch what he said.

"You sleeping okay?" the detective asked.

"Why? Someone spot me wandering around Portage Bay last night?"

"I'm just curious if you're sticking to that sleepwalking bullshit."

Clay did not respond. He did not have the energy. Besides, whatever answer he gave, the detective would follow it up with another question, followed by more questions until Clay stumbled over his words and said something regrettable. And given his exhaustion and lack of food, he needed to choose his words carefully. Silence, in the end, would serve him best.

The activity in the water increased as a second boat reached the spot of the divers. One of the officers at the end of the dock shouted and then waved for Detective Carpenter to come back down.

"If you want this story to be more than a brief in tomorrow's paper, you'll have to let me include a description of the body," Clay stated. "I'll also need some sort of official response on how this might be tied to those other murders."

"Fair enough. Let me check on what they found. I'll give you a call a little later."

"To push this with my editor, I need to know what I can use in the next hour."

The detective started to walk towards the dock. "Like I said, I'll call you later."

In the bay, the heads of the divers appeared and disappeared above the surface of the water, bobbing around like untethered black buoys. He should get back to the newsroom and give Melissa a summary of what he had found, he thought. That was the sensible thing to do. What he wanted to do, however, was go home and sleep the rest of the day.

The sky had turned a heavy gray. When he was young, in the summer months of June, July, and August, he loved to go to the top of the grassy hill at Gas Works Park, lie down, and watch the airplanes float across the crystal-clear sky. Closing his eyes, he would listen for the sound of the airplane. Sound always trailed light. Like now. Light and sound were out of synch. In those moments, like now, the world of his thoughts and the world of his senses seemed at odds, unreal and incomprehensible.

The drive to the newsroom proved difficult as Clay struggled to stay awake, his eyes drifting closed as he drove with scant awareness of the road. Sleep. What he would not give for a couple of hours of peaceful sleep.

With a jerk of his head, he found himself careening into oncoming traffic. Car horns blared. He swerved to the right, overcorrected, and quickly had to veer back to the left, the steering wheel nearly spinning from his grasp before he finally regained control. He immediately pulled over to the side of the road and turned off the car; he leaned his head against the steering wheel; he was going to kill himself if he did not sleep. A few moments passed as he caught his breath. He then reclined the driver's seat as far back as it would go, rolled onto his right side and closed his eyes. After a brief hesitation, he slipped into a deep unconsciousness.

Clay awoke to the sound of something loud knocking against the car. Dazed, he saw an elderly woman slapping the palm of her hand against the passenger-side window. She shouted something, but he could not make out the words above the smacking sounds on the glass. The time on his watch read 10:33. He had slept about fifteen minutes.

Clay brought his seat up to a sitting position. The woman's agitation increased.

"What?" Clay shouted.

"…park here!"

Clay raised his hands. "I can't understand?"

The woman appeared on the verge of hysterics. "You can't park here!" She then gestured to a sign that designated this spot for loading and unloading only.

"I've called the police. Do you hear me! The police!"

"I'm moving," Clay responded with a dismissive wave and started the car.

The woman continued to yell even as he pulled back into traffic.

Still exhausted, he traveled a couple of more blocks before finding another parking spot. This one did not appear to have any restrictions. He set the seat back down again and promised himself he would only sleep another ten minutes.

Entering the newsroom, Clay braced for the worst. The nap in the car had helped to clear his head, but it had also made him late. Melissa would be out for blood. At his desk, the computer monitor had three notes taped to it. Each note, written in Melissa's jagged cursive, had the time posted in the corner. The newer the note, the more hostile the tone: "See me when you get in." "Where are you!" The third note, which she had written ten minutes ago, had a message to call Detective Carpenter.

Before he could get the computer turned on, though, Melissa was marching towards him. As she reached his desk, she grabbed a nearby chair and sat uncomfortably close to him.

"Do you want me to fire you right now?" She spoke in a tight whisper, the veins in her neck flaring out under the strain.

"What…"

"You should have called or returned to the newsroom more than an hour ago. I should have already received your budget summary for the Portage Bay story.

The photographer has been back at least two hours. The morning meeting has come and gone, and I had nothing to give them except excuses. All the while, this story leads all the afternoon newscasts. And what do I have – not even a goddamn budget line!"

"I know. I'm sorry. I was trying to get some reaction from people living in the area," Clay lied.

"I don't want excuses. You do this again and I'm writing you up. Do I make myself clear?"

Clay's eyes dropped to the keyboard in front of him. From the outside, the gesture might have appeared submissive, but he was trying to control his anger, trying to avoid making the situation worse by lashing out at Melissa.

"What's going on with you anyway? You look like hell and you've been uncharacteristically sloppy at work. Clay? Look at me! I need you to stay sharp. We have a couple of reporters on vacation and I need you to pick up the slack. Am I being clear?"

"Yes, I get it!"

Melissa appeared to relax a bit after this. "So, what does the detective want?"

"Not sure. I talked to him at the crime scene. He thought the Portage Bay body might be tied to a series of other murders."

"Really?" Melissa smiled. "None of the television stations mentioned anything about that. Call him back and see if there's any truth to it. If there is, we still have a spot below the fold on the metro section."

Melissa stood up. "You have fifteen minutes to call the detective and write up a budget. If you can get information that this murder is tied to others, and we're the first to have it, I might forgo the written warning. But only if you give me something solid."

Clay punched in the detective's number, annoyed by Melissa's attempt at a threat. It was bullshit. He knew that. But it angered him anyway. The call went to voicemail.

He left a message and then wrote up a budget for the Portage Bay story that included the link to the three other murders. If the detective did not call back in the next few minutes, he planned to send the budget through. He also thought about writing the story whether the detective gave him the go-ahead or not. The constant cowing to the detective's control had grown tiresome.

12:48 p.m.

Kiki sat on the couch. She would have to leave for work soon. Her eyes scanned the apartment. It was a mess. The furniture was out of place, the couch still pushed against the front door. Books and papers spread haphazardly across the dining room table. Dirty clothes lay scattered around the living room since she no longer felt comfortable in the bedroom, even to get dressed. Dishes had piled up in the sink. The kitchen. She used to keep things clean and organized. Like her grandmother. She just didn't have the energy for any of that now.

On a more positive note, she had talked to the owner of the Pioneer Square building a half hour ago. The woman had been nice. She hadn't asked too many questions and had accepted Kiki's explanation about a family member who might have lived in the building. They planned to meet Saturday afternoon outside the building. The fact that she had a time set up to look around that old structure should have served as a distraction from everything else. It didn't. She kept thinking about the figure on the sidewalk; the rocks spelling out the word STOP; Nana's death; the attack; the antique journal. She considered, again, calling the police to explain the connection between these events, how someone had murdered her grandmother and was now harassing her. But the idea came and went. If the police had considered her unstable before, they might simply lock her up now. Was she crazy? It felt like it. Like she was lost in a dream in which every sound and movement made her muscles tense and her heart race.

Against the quiet, a soft humming sound began to vibrate through the apartment. One more hour before she could leave for the hospital. She preferred work. Anything was better than staying at the apartment. But it was difficult to leave. Leaving meant coming back. And coming back meant the possibility of someone waiting for her.

Kiki lay down on the couch and listened to the murmur of the melody as if it were coming from somewhere else. The rhythm so familiar. Like one of the traditional Duwamish songs Nana used to sing while she cleaned the house or cooked. Kiki wished she could remember the words. She knew a few Duwamish phrases, but none of the songs. The tune swirled off the surrounding walls, offering a rare moment of calm, a brief dislocation from her anger and fear.

Pre-dawn

The loamy taste of dirt filled Clay's mouth. The smell of tree sap scented the air. Slowly, he pushed himself up from the ground and scooted into a sitting position, leaning against the concrete foundation of a clapboard-sided building. It was cold. A cedar hedge blocked his view of the surrounding area. Clay closed and then opened his eyes as if that might settle his confusion as to where he was and why he was outside. A misty morning glow illuminated the quiet landscape. He still wore the faded-blue sweatpants and gray University of Washington sweatshirt he had put on before going to bed. His feet were bare. The scars did not appear to have reopened. No fresh blood.

The rough squawk of a crow echoed from a nearby tree.

Moving away from the wall, he crouched down and forced his way free of the hedge, brushing off cobwebs and broken cedar branches as he emerged onto the adjoining sidewalk. The cold, wet concrete sent a fresh chill through his body. With a clear view of the area, it only took a moment to understand where he was. During the night, he had walked the three and half miles to Eva's apartment building. Vague half-asleep, half-awake visions of the trek lingered in his head. He knew why he had walked here. There were things he needed to discuss with her. Unpleasant things. Subjects he wanted to avoid and wished he could put off indefinitely. He did not feel ready. Not yet. He did not want to be ready.

...long I stood there wondering, fearing,
Doubting, dreaming dreams no mortal ever dared to
dream...

Clay spat. The sour taste of dirt still hung in his mouth. From the angle of the emerging gray light, he guessed the time to be around eight in the morning. He should be home getting ready for work. A quick check of his pockets reassured him he had brought his keys. But there was no money for a cab. Not even a quarter to make a phone call. And despite having done it during the night, he had no intention of walking barefoot back to his apartment.

That left Eva. He could wake her up and explain why he had walked there in the middle of the night. Try to get her to understand what he needed her to do. Get her to see his side of the situation. His explanation, he feared, would only confuse her, and the conversation would morph into an argument; his anger would grow along with an urge for violence. She would not see the reasoning behind his actions. Nor would she cooperate. Clay's fingernails dug deep into the palms of his hands. He could go up to Eva's, not wake her up, and simply take money from her purse for a cab ride home. She would not know the difference; no argument; no violence.

Clay took several deep breaths. Indistinct images of walking in the dark flittered through his head. Hazy, unsettled thoughts. From the tall Douglas fir across the street a crow glided down to land in the middle of the road next to the body of a dead squirrel. The bird looked in Clay's direction and gave three loud squawks as if staking its sole claim to the dead animal.

117

Before opening the door, Clay listened the low hum of television voices coming from the apartment. The sound had a familiar, reassuring quality, as if there were still some benignly predictable aspects to the world.

He slid the key in the lock, turned the door's brass knob, stepped in, and carefully closing the door behind him even though he could have slammed it shut and not woken his mother up. As he started up the hallway, it became clear the sound of the television was coming from the living room and not the bedroom. He peeked in the bedroom and found it empty. In the living room, Eva lay face down at an awkward angle on the couch. At first, she did not appear to be breathing. But there it was. Movement. Her respiration came in slow, shallow breaths. Thai food spilled from a Styrofoam restaurant container on the coffee table. An empty red wine bottle sat next to it. Clay looked in the direction of the kitchen and saw that the mess he had cleaned up last week had already begun to return. His anger hardened. Not at his mother so much. At himself for thinking he could change anything by picking up her mess.

Clay turned off the television. Standing over Eva, he gave her body a not-so-gentle shake. "Mom?"

There was no reaction. He shook her harder and increased the volume of his voice. "Mom! Wake up!" She stirred. Her eyes, with a glazed, lost appearance, fluttered open. She looked from the fabric of the couch to Clay and then up towards the apartment ceiling.

"We need to talk!"

"What?" Her voice sounded weak, far away.

"I said we need to talk! Why are you on the couch?"

Eva made a feeble attempt to sit up, but only managed to roll onto her side. "What's going on?"

Eva's confusion tightened Clay's anger. He did not want to see her like this. Weak. Helpless. He found it difficult to breathe, as if the surrounding air lacked enough oxygen. "You're on the couch in the living room," he snapped. "It looks like you passed out watching TV."

Clay took her wrist and pulled her into a sitting position. The smell of stale alcohol hovered about her. Her eyes looked around with an air of sleepy uncertainty. "Why are you here?"

From where he stood, he could see a pot on the stove half filled with dried-out spaghetti.

"To check on you," he said. He did not expect her to hear his words, though. Did not care. He could have said anything and it would not have mattered. "You look horrible." Her skin had a jaundiced cast to it.

Eva lit a Benson and Hedges cigarette and leaned forward to reach the ashtray in the middle of the coffee table. Her hand shook. "Good morning to you, too, sunshine. You don't look all that put together, either," she said. "Where are your shoes?"

"Back at my apartment. I walked here."

"You what?"

He could have let her sleep. With the noise from the television, it would not have taken much to find her purse and take the money. She would have never woken up. And it would have saved him this unnecessary aggravation. "I'm sleepwalking. Remember? We talked about this last week. Do you remember me telling you that?"

"Yes, yes, I remember. But you walked here!"

"Yes, I walked here. And I'm going to need to borrow $20 for a cab home?"

Eva gave a sluggish wave of her hand in the direction of the kitchen. "There's cash in my purse on the counter there," she said.

She stood up, her balance unsteady.

Clay struggled against the impulse to grab her and force her to sit back down. He had not finished talking to her, and this made his anger flare at her getting up and walking away from him. "I understand you're going to

119

the Pioneer Square building." The words came out with a tight, irritated edge. He had walked here from his apartment to ask her this and it nevertheless felt pointless.

"Can we talk about this later, Clay? I'm not feeling well."

"No. This is a simple question!"

Eva started down the hallway. "I need to lie down." A hand went against the wall for support as she made it to the bathroom and shut the door with a loud clap. The muffled sound of vomiting soon followed.

Clay remained in the living room; his hands knuckled with his intensifying emotions. After a few minutes, the bathroom door opened; Eva stepped out and started down the hall to the bedroom. Clay caught up to her and grabbed her arm. "Are you going down to the Pioneer Square building on Saturday?"

Eva gave a cry of surprise at the sudden physical pain. "Let go, Clay! You're hurting my arm. What is wrong with you?"

He released her and took a step back. Eva stumbled, almost falling over, and then managed to make her way to the bedroom, slamming the door behind her. She was right. Something was wrong with him. Like a deep, cancerous disease that grew faster than he could control. He had tried to slow things down, to think his actions through and be more cautious. Less emotional. He needed to keep that in mind when he dealt with Eva. Her drinking had entered one of those dangerous, self-destructive phases he had experienced so many times growing up. He needed to take a more nuanced approach with her if he was going to keep her from turning against him.

He was in second grade the first time Eva entered rehab. Eva had overdosed on a mixture of prescription pills and alcohol. His parents were still married back then. He remembered how confused he had felt at seeing her at the treatment center, confused about why she had left home, confused about what had put her in this strange hospital. The treatment center sat on several well-manicured acres. The main building was a refurbished mansion. The marble-white building stood three stories tall with Doric columns across the front portico. Flowers and ferns, rhododendron and fruit trees dotted the surrounding grounds as if to reacquaint the residents with the idea of an earthly paradise.

On the family visits to the treatment center, Eva was sober and clear headed, engaged and focused in way that felt foreign. She laughed and smiled with an unfeigned ease. She asked each of the three kids how things were going and then quietly listened to the excited responses. Eva even introduced them to one of the other patients, a friend she had made at the facility who called himself Peter Pan. He was young with short, blond hair, and a thin, wiry frame; he had a high, singsong voice and always seemed in a state of great animation. For a time, Clay imagined this young man might actually *be* Peter Pan with his effeminate demeanor that made Eva laugh so easily. She had started painting again while in rehab and commented that she and Peter Pan were the asylum's artists in residence.

Clay went over and tamped out the still-smoking cigarette; he then took a seat on the couch. The overflow of stress and anxiety made it difficult to think or move. There was not much of a point in trying to wake Eva up again. He still needed to know about the upcoming visit to the Pioneer Square building. He needed to hear it from her. To be certain. But that wasn't going to happen. Not right now.

With nothing to do but grow more frustrated, Clay went to the phone and called for a taxi. The dispatch said it would take about thirty minutes to arrive.

He opened the two living room windows. The light morning breeze brought in some much-needed fresh air. In the kitchen, he found a newly opened box of trash bags, took one out, and filled it with food containers and glass bottles.

2:16 p.m.

Clay picked up his work phone and dialed Eva's number. Again. The ringing sounded far away. This was the third call since getting to work. Or maybe it was the fourth. Eva had yet to answer. If she did not answer, he would go to her apartment in person. Ringing. More ringing. She was not going to pick up. The answering machine clicked on and he let his head drop. He had already left a message. He hung up the phone and slumped back in his chair, staring at the blinking screen of the word processor.

"Clay?"

He sat up and looked in the direction of Melissa's office. "Do you have the piece on the Capital Hill perfume thefts ready yet?"

"Just finishing with your edits."

"Have you requested art?"

"I'll do that now."

Melissa approached his desk. "You look like hell."

"I'm fine. Just some trouble sleeping," he said.

"Sleeping pills, Clay. It's not complicated. Throw in a shot of vodka and it's like Hypnos himself has blessed you."

"I'll try to remember that," Clay replied and then picked up the phone to call the photography department.

Clay's tightly wound thoughts vibrated within the high-pitched whine of the four-cylinder engine as he headed for Madison Park. The need to talk to Eva had grown into something frantic. If she had just answered the goddamn phone, he could have avoided this! He worried the visit to the Pioneer Square building might have been today, which only intensified his agitation. Things were so jumbled. He might be wrong; he could still stop her and avoid acting on other considerations, other unpleasant notions and actions that grated at the edges of his thoughts like a festering infection, goading him towards something violent, something at odds with who he thought he should be, who he wanted to be.

A light rain tapped against the windshield. Part of him, the last remaining calm and sensible part, urged him to go home and let his thoughts rest for a short time. To sleep. The exhaustion kept him from thinking clearly. And he knew that. But he was afraid of where he might go if he slept. All day he had shuffled through various options on how to avoid another night of wandering around. The sleeping pills had not helped. The anxiety medication had done little to calm his mood. If he did go home, he thought about setting his alarm to go off every half hour. Or maybe every fifteen minutes. If he kept himself from entering a deep sleep, he reasoned, if he kept waking up after a short interval, he would not have time to leave the apartment. That was the idea, at least.

He had also called the doctor's office with the vague idea of making an appointment to ask for a new course of treatment. He had no idea of what that might entail. He needed something else. Perhaps the doctor could prescribe a new drug. Or a breathing exercise. The earliest appointment, though, would not be for another three weeks. It would be too late by then.

It took several minutes to find a parking spot once he reached Eva's neighborhood. He prepared for the fact that she might already be drunk; or she might yell at him for waking her up so early that morning; or she might not be there at all. Whatever the case, he needed to stay calm and maintain control.

With the car turned off, he sat in the quiet and wished he had more benzos. The medication he had brought to work was long gone. He toyed with the idea of going home, medicating himself, and then coming back to Eva's place. But he was parked. He did not want to move. Everything became quiet but for the tapping of the rain on the metal roof of the car; the evening sky had faded into night.

He forced himself to get out of the car after sitting there for some time. He did not bother to put up his hood. At the building's entrance, out of habit, he rang the buzzer to Eva's apartment. To his surprise, she answered.

"Yes, Clay?"

The fact that she knew it was him produced an uncomfortable laugh. "How did you know it was me?"

"What do you want?"

"You weren't answering your phone. I wanted to make sure you're okay."

"Why wouldn't I be okay?"

He hesitated, reminding himself not to argue with her out here on the street. "Do you remember me coming by this morning?" He waited. There was no response. "Are you still there?"

"Yes, I remember. I also got your message. I don't need a babysitter, Clay."

"I know. Is it all right if I come up? I need to talk to you."

"I'm not discussing my drinking..."

"That's not what I want to talk about."

And with that, the front door buzzed, and Clay went in. He found her door ajar when he reached the fourth floor. Inside, the apartment smelled of recently sprayed chemical air-freshener.

Eva sat on the couch in the living room. Smoke rose from a cigarette in the ashtray on the coffee table. Next to the ashtray, Eva had neatly arranged three magazines and a newspaper in the shape of a fan as if to declare this a world of order and balance. She did not look up when he walked in. Her eyes remained focused on an art magazine in her hands. She wore an orange blouse and jeans. Her hair appeared recently combed. Looking around, he noticed she had cleaned. No alcohol. Not that he could see. Steam rose from a teapot on the kitchen stove.

"How are you feeling?" he asked.

"Fine." She closed the magazine and set it down with the others on the coffee table. Eva stood up and took a dirty plate into the kitchen. "If you are here to lecture me, Clay, I'm not interested," she said, irritation coloring her voice.

"No lectures. But you could help me understand why I found you passed out on the couch this morning." He stayed in the living room, somewhat relieved to see her tend to the water on the stove and not pouring a drink.

"I wasn't passed out. I sometimes fall asleep in the living room. Not sure why I need to explain that to you."

"What about all the liquor and wine bottles and the mess in the kitchen?"

"Enough! Let me repeat what I said earlier: if you came here to lecture me, you can leave!"

Clay raised his hands. "Okay. Sorry. I'm done."

"Things are a little difficult right now." She put a tea bag in a mug and filled it with water from the pot on the stove. "I'm doing my best to work through it."

Clay thought about sitting down but felt too anxious. "Work through what?"

"It's nothing, Clay." Eva returned to the living room. "Nothing I want to discuss right now. You said you wanted to talk. What is it?" She took a seat on the couch and set the cup of tea on the table.

"You said you were going to the Pioneer Square building and you never explained why."

A look of confusion crossed her face. "When did I tell you that?"

"This morning," he lied. The lies, even to his mother, like all the other assorted lies, happened with such ease now. No forethought. No need to plan.

"Did I?"

"Yes. When are you going?" Clay felt his patience slipping with each additional question.

"Saturday."

"You said you were meeting someone."

"I honestly don't remember this conversation."

Clay tilted his head up at the ceiling and attempted to control the anger and irritability wrestling to punch past the façade of calm. "Why are you going down there?" The volume of his voice rose.

"It's nothing mysterious, Clay. I got a call from the real estate company that manages the building. A woman contacted them with questions about the building's his–"

"Have you talked to this woman?"

"She called a couple days ago. She thinks a relative might have lived in the building and wanted to know if she could look around. What is this all about?"

"Are you meeting with her?"

Eva took a drink of tea. "Yes, like I said, I'm meeting with her on Saturday."

"You need to cancel." The snap in his voice made Eva look up. "You need to call her back and tell her you can't meet with her."

"And why would I do that?"

Clay considered this for a moment. The lie needed to sound reasonable, to form a string of benign words that would smooth out the violent tone of his voice. "It's not safe."

"What's not safe?" she asked. "The woman is researching her family's past. I hardly think an interest in genealogy is a cause for alarm. Besides, it's in the middle of the day, in one of the busiest parts of the city."

"I'm asking you, please, to not meet with her. I have concerns about this that are difficult to explain."

"If you're that worried about my safety, come with me?"

Clay shook his head and looked at his hands. He was afraid to speak, afraid of the words that would leave his mouth. "I can't," he finally said. "I have things at work I need to do."

"Come on, Clay. It'll be good for you to get away from work and out of your apartment for a while, and, who knows, maybe you and this woman might hit it off. She sounded very nice on the phone. Besides, when was the last time you dated? Or not even that, when was the last time you went out and did something relaxing?"

Clay sat down in the brightly colored orange and yellow armchair. His hands rubbed against his pants. He watched the curling smoke rise from the cigarette on the table. "I have too much going on," he said. She was not listening, though. Did not seem to hear him. "It would make things so much easier if you didn't go," he mumbled.

But Eva had continued to talk as if he hadn't said anything. "...this morning, why do I recall you not wearing shoes?"

The magazines on the table gave the space the pretense of calm and control. Like a theatrical show. He needed something like that. An appearance of order and restraint. It just felt impossible to explain to Eva what was happening in a way that would not make her want to call the police and have him locked up. "I walked here." The words came out in a flat, even cadence. That was good. To maintain an impression of composure even as his hands chafed against the fabric of his pants.

"Barefoot? That doesn't make any sense..."

"Sense?" Clay laughed through clenched teeth. "You are right! Good job! It doesn't make any sense. What part of walking in my fucking sleep is supposed to make

128

sense!" The angry words echoed through the room. "I need you to stop talking for a minute and listen. I sleep about forty-five minutes a night. The rest of the time, I'm wandering all over the fucking city like a goddamn zombie! Do you understand what I'm saying? Does that make sense?"

"Yes, Clay, I hear what you're saying. Please, calm down." There was a quiver of fear in her voice. "Have you made a doctor's appointment like I suggested?"

He struggled to change the tone of his voice. "The earliest appointment wasn't for a couple of weeks."

"Go to another doctor, then. You need help. The things you're doing aren't safe..."

Clay looked towards the ceiling and laughed. Safe? What does safe have to do with anything?

"...get yourself killed."

"I know." It already felt like it was too late. He fought the urge to explain how the sleepwalking and violent thoughts and feelings were all connected and not something he could easily untangle.

"...help me understand." Her voice came out soft and compliant as she continued to talk. "...medication..." Her voice never seemed to stop.

"I don't need more pills." He stood up. "My problem isn't a lack of medication. The problem is letting strangers root around in our family business. That's the goddamn problem!"

Eva held up her hands. "It's okay, Clay. Nothing bad is going to happen from this. She just wants to look around. There's nothing but dust and empty space in that building."

"I need to go," he said, his fists balled up tight. If he stayed, his last bit of control would slip away and then anything was possible.

Eva spoke more words, but the sounds no longer carried any meaning. He started down the hallway to leave. Eva moved to stop him; he brushed past her, knocking her into the wall. He needed to get home. Needed to take something to settle his nerves. Needed to get away from here, away from himself.

Early Morning

Clay!

The sound crackled like radio static. Far away. Difficult to understand. A flash of bright light hit his eyes and mixed with spots of damp darkness. Movement and sound flickered at the edges; the act of processing all of it came slow, steeped in a chemical fog.

Another clap of sound filled the air. "Clay!"

And as the world came into focus, it wasn't the glare of the light or the anger in the voice that stood out, but the loud, stereophonic quality of the rain. It surrounded him. He was outside. Again. Yet again. Through the chaotic movement of the light, he found himself kneeling in the damp earth. Mud caked his hands. To his left stood the figure with the flashlight. The man took ahold of Clay's shirt. The beam of light bobbed from Clay's face to the underside of an evergreen tree branch above. He felt himself being lifted.

"What is wrong with you? Get up!"

Clay recognized the angry baritone of the detective's voice. He swung out an arm and managed to knock himself free from the man's grasp; the momentum of the movement sent Clay falling backwards onto the ground.

"Are you high?" The detective took another tight grip on Clay's shirt and tried again to hoist him to his feet.

Clay could hear the rain tapping against the branches overhead. His clothes and hair were soaked.

"Clay!" The detective's voice held a mix of anger and disbelief. "If you don't respond in the next five seconds, I'm going to throw you in the car and dump you at Harborview as a drug overdose. Do you understand?"

Clay took hold of the detective's hand and pushed it away. "I understand!" The words came out in a slow slur. "What the hell are you doing?"

The detective said something, but the sounds blended with the noise of the rain. Clay felt sick. Dizzy. "What?"

The flashlight had steadied. It now shone directly in Clay's face. He brought a hand up to shield his eyes.

"Do you know where you are?" the detective demanded.

"Outside. In the rain." Clay did little to suppress the mocking tone of his response. He had a good idea of where he was.

The detective gave a clipped laugh. "Right. What I'm asking is if you know where, geographically, you are right now?"

Clay remained quiet.

"Okay, let me explain it to you, then. It's two o'clock in the goddamn morning and here you are out wandering Volunteer Park!"

Clay shivered as a light breeze disturbed the air. "Why are you here?"

"Really? That's the question you want to ask? If it were me, I'd be wondering why I'm wandering around Volunteer Park in the middle of the night."

Clay brushed his dirty hands on his sweatpants. With the sleeve of his shirt, he wiped his runny nose. "How did you find me?"

"I followed you."

Clay tried not to look surprised, but having the detective here changed things, made everything more difficult.

"Are you drunk?"

"No. It's the medications I take. The sleeping pills and things."

"So," the detective stated in a careful voice, "this is the sleepwalking bullshit you talked about. Is that the story you're going to tell me?"

Clay shrugged. He did not care what the detective thought. Did not care about any of that. What he cared about was getting him away from this spot.

"From where I was standing, you didn't look asleep. You seemed to have a pretty good idea of what you were doing and where you were going."

"Remind me again why you followed me?"

The detective had moved the beam of the flashlight to illuminate the area in front of Clay. "A call came in about someone walking around 12th Avenue in pajamas and no shoes. I was in the area and said I would check on it. And guess what? I found you looking as though you were headed somewhere important," the detective said.

There was very little to see beyond the small glow of the flashlight. "Why didn't you stop me?"

"You disappeared into the park before I could chase you down."

Struggling against the fog of medications and alcohol, Clay found it difficult to scheme a way out of this without making the detective more curious. "How did you find me here?"

"After I parked and started walking around, I heard what sounded like arguing. I followed the noise and found you down on your knees tearing at the ground and having a heated disagreement with yourself."

"Digging?"

"Like a damn dog. I thought you'd gone crazy. Look," the detective said and pointed the flashlight at a

133

spot of ground a couple of feet from where Clay knelt. The light illuminated a small bowl-shaped hole.

"What was I saying?"

"Hell if I know. I couldn't make out a single word. To be honest, I was afraid someone would hear you, and I did not want to explain to the swing shift how you and I ended up in the woods of Volunteer Park with you crying out like a stuck pig."

"You couldn't understand anything?" Clay asked. In the faint, unsteady light, he stared at his dirt-stained hands.

"Why? You have some dark secret you only reveal in the middle of the night while digging holes?"

Clay shook his head. Nevertheless, that was exactly what he feared – that he had let slip something that needed to remain hidden.

The detective moved closer to the shallow hole. The beam showed nothing more than dark earth and a tangled filigree of thin roots.

"What were you digging for?" the detective asked.

Clay's shoulder muscles tightened. The detective was going to turn this into an interrogation. Clay tried to think of a way to leave before man asked any more questions. "I don't know," he responded, but even he could hear the lie in those three simple words.

The detective knelt next to the depression. "You cold?"

"What?"

"You're shaking. Are you cold?"

Clay laughed. "What do you think? I'm soaked, no shoes, it's the middle of the night. Yes, I'm fucking cold."

"No need for attitude," the detective responded. "I'll grab a blanket for you when we get back to the car. But, and I'll be honest, that sleepwalking thing you keep blaming is the craziest shit I've ever heard." The detective dug at the hole with the butt of the flashlight. "You really don't know what you were digging for?"

Clay pushed himself to his feet. His legs ached and the bottom of his feet stung from what he guessed were fresh cuts. "No idea."

The detective grumbled something under his breath and then looked back up at Clay. "What do you say we dig a little deeper and see if anything is down there? If you help me out, I'll drive you home. Sound like a deal?"

No. That was the answer Clay wanted to give. There was nothing buried beneath the dirt he wished to share with the detective. "I'd rather go home and sleep," he said, doing little to hide his irritation. "Don't suppose you can take me home and then come back?"

The detective stood up and brushed the dirt from his pants. "Let's dig first," he said. "I just need to get the shovel out of the car."

"You have a shovel?"

"Of course. When people want to hide something, their first instinct is to bury it." He looked around. "I think I can find my way back. You going to wait here?"

Clay nodded. He then watched the flashlight sway with the irregular motion of the detective's walk as he headed up a nearby dirt trail, the narrow beam of light illuminating the trunks of trees, large ferns, rhododendrons. A breeze disturbed the overhanging branches and sent a shower of rainwater down on top of Clay. The shivering increased, from both the cold and his thinly stretched nerves. He tried to think of this moment as a dream, something unreal, a world he would soon leave once he woke up.

When the circular glow of the flashlight made its way back, Clay's shaking had intensified, and his teeth chattered. The detective carried a fold-up green army shovel that looked like a toy in his large hands. He tossed Clay a coarse wool blanket. "Aren't you a little curious about what you were digging up?" the detective asked.

"Not really." He draped the blanket over his shoulders. The shaking only seemed to grow more violent. Maybe the detective would not find anything, he thought in a weak attempt to calm his agitation. "I sometimes dream about being at the beach and digging in the sand. Maybe I was doing that."

"I don't know," the detective responded. "The tone of your argument didn't suggest playing at the beach. Besides that, you seemed to know exactly where you wanted to dig."

The detective handed Clay the flashlight and moved over to the shallow hole. "Shine the light on where I'm digging, please," he said. Clay had turned the light upwards to look at the overhanging tree branches.

The wet earth was soft, and the few roots the detective encountered offered little resistance. The surrounding trees dampened the sound of the detective's work, giving it a flat, echoless quality that made it feel like the two men stood within a closed space.

"Why are you out so late?" Clay asked, intently watching each shovel full of dirt the detective tossed aside.

"I'm always out late. Don't need much sleep, and the overtime pay helps cover the cost of my ex-wife's lavish lifestyle. And, besides, I don't do well sitting at home doing nothing."

"Have you found Redman?"

"Nope. Damn kid has disappeared. I'm thinking he's laying low until this Watts character is gone. That's what I'm hoping, at least."

The detective then straightened and tapped the tip of the shovel against an object that gave a hollow metallic ring.

"I think we found something."

Clay stepped closer. The hole was about a foot and a half deep.

"Hold that damn light steady," the detective snapped. He leaned over and cleared away some more of the dirt with his hands. "Looks like we have a box of some sort."

Clay dropped to a knee and put the light next to the detective's hand. With his finger, the detective worked around the edges of a rectangular piece of rusted metal.

"What in the hell did you bury?" The detective grabbed the shovel and worked the tip down next to one of the sides, easily prying loose a shoebox-sized container from the dirt. The contents of the box shifted and made a grating sound of metal against metal. Large areas of rust spotted the container's gray surface. No lock. Only a stainless-steel clasp.

The detective popped the box open. "Will you look at that?" A deep, low laugh emerged from the large man. "A jewelry collection. What do girls call this…a hope chest? Is that what this is?"

Clay ignored the detective's mocking tone. The light of the flashlight reflected off an assortment of variously colored pieces of jewelry: rings, bracelets, some necklaces, earrings. There were also a couple of old military medals and several larger men's rings. Tarnish dulled most of the items; a few, however, looked relatively new.

With an oversized index finger, the detective poked around among the different gold, silver, and copper objects. "Some of these look like they've been in here for a while," he commented. He picked up a thick ring that had a gold triangular symbol set against a purple background. There was a small gem at the center. "Do you suppose that's a real diamond?"

"I have no idea." The sight of the ring made Clay uncomfortable and anxious, forcing him to resist the urge to grab it from the detective's hand.

"So what is all this stuff?" the detective asked, putting the ring back. "Or are you going to feed me more crap about sleepwalking amnesia?"

A sense of relief settled over Clay at not seeing the detective holding the ring. "They're just family pieces."

137

He took out a gold filigree-styled ring that had a large gold nugget at its center. The ring had an antique patina darkening various points across the surface. "This was my grandmother's."

"Okay. So, explain to me again why it's here?"

Clay shrugged. "I must have put it here. But I have no idea why, or even how long any of this has been in that box."

"Why do I have such a hard time accepting your sleepwalking bullshit?" the detective said with a stern look at Clay.

"This necklace is my mom's. So are these earrings."

The detective sat back on the wet ground and shook his head. "You know how crazy this sounds? I mean it. Do you? You expect me to believe you not only sleepwalk, but you also bury treasure in the woods of Volunteer Park?"

Clay continued to pick up different pieces and inspect them. There must have been close to sixty different items in the box.

"You really don't remember putting any of this here?"

"No." Clay took out a silver ring with a dime-sized, oval piece of citrine. Scratches and discoloration marked the silver of the ring. His great grandmother had owned this. The ring had been one of the first pieces he had collected.

The detective stood and brushed himself off. He picked the shovel up and poked around in the hole a little more. "I have half a mind to take that box with me and give it a good run-through."

"What?" The idea of the detective taking the box was unacceptable. That was not going to happen. "Why? You think this stuff is stolen?"

"Well, is it?"

With a grating metallic noise, Clay agitated the box, moving the different pieces around to get a better view of it all. "No, like I said, this is all stuff from my family." He picked out a silver necklace with a half-inch medallion of polished turquoise. "I'm not sure what my mom would say if she knew I'd buried all these things here, but I doubt she'd press charges."

"Then you have nothing worry about. Let me take it with me. I'll return it in a couple of days."

Clay closed the lid and set the clasp back into place. The box was going to stay with him. "No, I should go over this stuff with my mom to figure out what belongs to who. Tell you what, if there's anything in here we don't recognize, I'll forward that on to you."

"I suppose," the detective said. He dug around the hole a little longer, then took the flashlight from Clay and started back up the winding dirt trail.

Evening

Gray twilight weighed against the crimson bricks of the apartment building. Sitting in his car, Clay wished he had somewhere else to go. Anywhere. He had spent most of Saturday at the newsroom working on the crime statistics story. Not that he cared much about the story anymore; he just needed an excuse to get out of the apartment and stop thinking about Eva's trip to the Pioneer Square building.

He thought about the inevitability of sleep. The previous night he had the alarm go off every twenty minutes. And while that had kept him from wandering out of the apartment, it had left him profoundly exhausted. And it showed. He could see it in his reflection. His hair was unkempt, as if he had just woken up. The area under his eyes was puffy and discolored; the lines across his forehead and around his mouth appeared deep and intractable. He had not eaten. Not that he could remember, at least. His face held a gaunt, hollow appearance. Almost unrecognizable. Like a stranger battling a debilitating illness.

Once inside the apartment, he knew, it would be hard to do anything but sleep. He rested the back of his hand against the driver-side window, the glass surface cold against his skin, a comforting counterpoint to his heated, un-trackable thoughts. A couple walked by, and Clay grew conscious of the fact he had been sitting here for some time. He opened the car door and made the short walk to the building.

The apartment felt pleasantly warm compared to the drizzly chill outside. He tossed his keys on the kitchen counter. Opening the refrigerator, he stared at the mostly empty shelves, eventually taking out the carton of eggs. There were three left.

Standing at the stove, he listened to the sound of the rain outside. He picked at a sore on his arm, causing it to open up and bleed. He felt so tired. It took considerable effort to take out a pan and place it on one of the coiled electric burners. Was he even hungry? He should eat. That much seemed true. He could quickly scramble a couple of eggs. The sound of the rain, however, grew louder, and his energy to cook diminished.

He left the stove and went to the bedroom to take off his shoes. His fingers felt swollen and uncoordinated as he fumbled with the laces. He thought of his mom and wished he had done a better job of explaining how bad things had gotten and how critical it was that she cancel the trip downtown.

In the silence, it almost sounded as if Eva were calling his name, like when he was little and the family still lived at the Eastlake house. He would be upstairs in his room and she would yell up at him from the ground floor when she needed something. There was a particularly high, piercing pitch she achieved that made it impossible to ignore her. It used to drive him crazy. Now the memory of her strained voice made him long for that lost time. Here, in the windowless bedroom, everything felt quiet. No sound of rain or traffic. Only indistinct noises pinging through his head. What was wrong? He brought a trembling hand to his face. Like the world had stumbled from its axis. His hands. His face. He fought the urge to lie down. If he could rest without fear of going outside, he would let himself sleep for days. His eyes drifted close; he made a vague promise to only rest for a moment, a minute or two.

When Clay awoke, his eyes focused on the white, textured ceiling, the glow of the bedroom light. He could not tell how long he might have slept. His eyes drifted closed again, and his muscles relaxed so that it felt like floating. Then came the ring of the phone. It might have already been ringing. He did not move. His eyes opened. He listened to the phone and debated whether he had the energy to get up and answer it. The ringing eventually stopped, and the answering machine clicked on. It was Eva's voice. He pushed himself up from the bed. He had called several times, leaving at least one message, in order to question her about the meeting at the Pioneer Square building.

He reached the phone just as she was finishing her message. "Hello… Hello… Don't hang up. Hello?"

"Clay?"

"Yes, just a second. Let me turn the answering machine off." With a little bit of fumbling he managed to stop the recorder. "Sorry about that."

"I'm returning your call," Eva said. "The two messages you left have me a little worried. Are you okay?"

"I'm fine. The woman, did you meet with her?" A surge of anxious energy filled his voice to the point where he had to keep from shouting into the phone.

"Yes, Clay. I hope you're not going to argue with me about this again."

"Did she find anything?"

"This wasn't a treasure hunt. She was just doing some research and thought a family mem–"

"You told me that. I want to know if she found anything!"

"You should have come down, Clay. She was very nice."

He struggled to keep his voice in check, to not let his anger flare. "What did she find?" he asked again.

"I don't know about finding anything, but we discovered that the cellar of the building incorporates part of a pre-Seattle-fire structure."

"What makes you say that?"

"If you're so interested in this, why didn't you come down yourself?"

He ignored the question. "I want to know," he said, "what makes you think the cellar was part of an older building?"

"We found some initials and some dates carved into a couple of the bricks down there."

"What were the initials?"

"TP, I think."

Clay shook his head. "No, that doesn't sound right," he mumbled. "Was it AP?"

"I don't know. It was hard to tell given the age. You're welcome to go check for yourself."

Clay went quiet as he thought about the initials, forgetting his mother on the other end of the line. He needed to formulate a plan on how he would handle this. A way to shut all of it down.

"…can't understand…"

"Are you meeting with her again?"

"What is going on with you? She was a very nice young woman trying to track down some family history."

"Are you meeting with her again?" he shouted.

"Settle down, Clay. I'm not going to continue this conversation…"

"Will you just answer the question, please?" Clay asked, making a concerted effort to moderate the tone of his voice.

"No, we don't have any plans to meet again." She then got after him for yelling at her and asked if he had made an appointment to see a doctor. Had the doctor's office understood how poorly he felt? Was he getting any sleep?

After a momentary pause to calm himself down, he apologized for the outburst and explained his system of setting the alarm to go off every twenty minutes to avoid any more sleepwalking. Things were getting better, he said. She did not need to worry. Instead of dropping the issue, Eva's lecture shifted to criticizing his attempts to help himself.

"…deprivation can cause hallucinations and depression and all sorts…"

"Okay." He wanted her to stop talking, her words coming and going without carrying any meaning. "Yes, I understand," he responded. He thought about hanging up the phone, but then Eva said something that made him pay attention.

"What was that?" he asked.

"I found a couple of boxes in the basement."

He felt his anxiety spike. "Boxes of what?"

"Family-related items. Some newspaper clippings, books, business documents, personal notes—"

"Did she see any of this?"

"See any of it? Why are you making such a big deal over …"

"Did she go through the boxes?" His anger and impatience surged again, easily brushing aside the feigned calm.

"Jesus, Clay! Yes, she did. Why does it matter?"

Clay took a couple of deep breaths. This changed things. "It would have been better if she hadn't gone through that stuff," he said, the words intended more for himself than Eva.

"What are you talking about?"

"You wouldn't understand," Clay said.

"You're right, I don't understand. Please explain it to me?"

"Where are the boxes?"

144

"I brought them home."

"I'll be over later to pick them up," he said.

Eva started to talk, but Clay hung up the phone, unsure if he had even said goodbye. Not that it mattered; not that he cared. There was too much to think about now. He unplugged the answering machine and pulled the cord from the phone. No more calls. No more disruptions. He sat down on the couch. Maybe it was the lack of sleep, or the need for food, but he felt ill. The palms of his hands came up and pushed against the soft tissue of his eyes, transforming the black to red. He felt nauseous. Sick. With the releasing of the pressure, black dots danced sporadically across his vision.

At the far end of the room, he focused on a black and white photograph that hung on the wall. The image showed a crowded street corner. Nearly all the people in the shot were blurred, indistinct men and women, most dressed in business suits and skirts, appearing as variously shaded streaks of gray. The only discernable figure was an elderly woman, just to the left of center. She sat on a bench. Perhaps tired from a walk. Or maybe she was panhandling. It was hard to tell. Her face had a slight smear to it, but nothing like the distortion of those around her. The crowd swept past her like a river around a stone. Clay had taken the photograph a couple of years ago. He liked that the woman sat so still among the blur of cars and agitated pedestrians, everyone too busy to stop and absorb what was happening around them.

Clay stood. He needed fresh air. He poured cold coffee into a mug and drank the bitter liquid in three quick swallows in the hope it might keep him awake.

Had he told Eva a time when he would pick up the boxes? He could not remember. All that forgetting. It made it difficult to answer even the simplest of questions, such as what day it was. Sunday? Did it matter? The day? There was so much to forget. So many things he needed to forget. He opened the door to the apartment and walked out. Thoughts came and went. Each thought more tortured than the last, all of them difficult to sort through and understand.

3:00 a.m.

The inability to breathe snapped Kiki awake. She couldn't move. Panic surged through her. A heavy weight pressed down on her arms and chest and a hand clamped over her mouth. She struggled. The pressure increased. The hand pushed down on her face and sank her head deep into the soft feather pillow. She couldn't breathe, her body convulsing against the restraints.

Then came sound. A voice. The words tangled with her muffled screams as the weight on her head and chest grew. An angry male voice came out in loud, quick bursts.

"...screaming! Stop...listen!"

And she tried to listen, to hear him, to stop, but it was all adrenaline and fear rushing through her.

"...all of it...understand!...you don't stop, I'll come back ..."

Kiki heard the word "understand" and moved her head as if to acknowledge her acceptance, to accept whatever she was supposed to understand, but the movement was met with more pressure and more anger. Soon, the man's words turned to sounds without meaning. She couldn't breathe. She was going to die. Like being rolled up in a heavy carpet and thrown into deep water.

"...doesn't change anything."

Her need to breathe grew more desperate.

"...understand!"

She kicked. Her eyes stayed wide open to the room's darkness, to the shapeless figure looming over her.

"…continue…if that happens…"

And then, all at once, the weight lifted, and air poured into her lungs. A twisted mass of blanket and sheets entombed her as she struggled to free herself, certain he was coming back to kill her even as she heard the apartment door open and shut. In those frightening moments, she wasn't sure if he had left or had just come back in, her panic giving her a confused sense of time, the rush of adrenaline making it hard to focus. Hard to hear. She wriggled into a sitting position and untangled from the rest of the covers. There was no sound. She listened. She tried to slow her thoughts and her breathing enough to hear anything that might indicate someone was still in the apartment. Everything remained quiet. She brought her feet to the floor. Still no sound. She moved from the bed and crept into the living room. Nothing. She flipped on every light switch she passed until she reached the apartment door, locked it, and then pushed the couch back in front of it.

Even then, she felt his presence hovering in the room. Could smell the rain and dirt his hands had ground into her face. Kiki picked up the phone and dialed 911. She kept her back to the wall so she could see the rest of the apartment. Part of her, surprisingly, remained unnaturally calm. When the operator answered and asked where the emergency was, Kiki gave her address and apartment number in a flat, unhurried manner. It felt like someone else was talking. The other part of her, the emotional portion of her, had entered a state of collapse. The operator asked her name. Kiki answered. The operator asked if the suspect was still present? Had she been injured? Kiki answered no. No.

"He held me down," she heard her voice explain when the operator asked if any weapons were involved.

The words, her words, evoked only the slightest of tremors.

"Did he assault you?"

She wasn't sure.

"Were you physically or sexually assaulted?"

"I don't know. His hand was over my mouth and nose. I couldn't breathe."

The questions flowed on like this for what felt like a long time. And because Kiki answered no to so many of the questions, she grew afraid the operator didn't consider her situation an emergency.

"How long is it going to be before someone comes?" she asked.

"It could be an hour or more. Officers are responding to several other calls right now."

"What should I do?"

"Lock the door and wait."

"How will I know it's a police officer?"

"They'll identify themselves."

"What if he comes back and says he's the officer?"

"Before you open the door, call 911 and get verification from dispatch of the officer's name and badge number."

When the call ended, Kiki found herself shaking and felt tears slide down her face. There was no sound of crying, though. No sound at all. It didn't feel real. Even the emergency operator had raised questions about whether any of it had happened, asking Kiki more than once if she had been drinking or taking drugs. No, Kiki had answered. How did he get in? the operator had asked. Kiki didn't know. The door had a new lock. She had even pushed the couch against the door before going to bed. None of that had kept him out, though, Kiki said. The noise from the couch scraping across the floor should have woken her up. It just didn't seem possible. Not the couch. Not the new lock. He had entered anyway. And he would be back. She remembered that. There wasn't much

149

else she could remember about what he had said. But she remembered his promise to come back.

Afternoon

Clay, I'm just asking how Mom looked when you saw her, Margaret said. "There's no reason to be defensive."

He wished he had not answered the phone. "I'm not being defensive." When it rang, he thought it was Melissa to rebuke him for calling out sick. It had taken him several moments to register his sister's voice. At first, he welcomed the call and the possibility of a mild distraction. But, instead, she wanted to talk about Eva and force him back in the direction of everything he wanted to forget. He considered hanging up the phone. Did it matter to have one more person angry with him? He was not particularly close with his sister. They rarely talked anymore. Growing up, especially after their parents' divorce, the two of them had looked out for and protected each other. That time, however, felt very long ago and nearly forgotten.

"When did you see her?"

"A day ago. Two days ago. I'm not sure."

"Did you go to her apartment?"

"Yes."

"And everything looked fine? She looked fine? The apartment?"

He had spent the last couple of days rummaging through the boxes of family papers he had picked up from Eva. "Things were out of place, I guess," he said. He focused on the sound of Margaret's voice, hoping the tone and inflection of her words would have a calming effect. "I did some dishes and took out the garbage. That sort of thing. She seemed a little hung over."

"You can't clean up her messes, Clay. You know that, don't you? It doesn't help. All you're doing is making it worse. She needs to take some responsibility. And, come on, I bet she was more than a little hung over."

"Have you seen her?"

"Today, we were supposed to meet for lunch, and she never showed up. Didn't call. Nothing. I waited at the restaurant for an hour. She wasn't answering her phone, either, so I went to her place and found her already drunk. One in the afternoon and she could barely make it to the door."

Clay wanted his voice to sound surprised, as if he were hearing this news for the first time, but the lie felt too empty and unimportant. "Okay. Why are you calling me?"

"Why? Because I hoped you might be a little concerned. She needs to go back into treatment. She doesn't look healthy. She isn't keeping her apartment clean. And I want the three of us, you, me, and Boyd, to sit down and confront her…"

For the first time, Clay noticed the blinking red light on the answering machine. He did not remember missing a call, but he had been dozing on and off all morning. He wondered if it might be Melissa, or possibly the detective. The thought of either of them leaving a message, however, accelerated his anxiety.

"What time is it?" Clay asked.

"A little past two."

That sounded about right given the gray light visible through the narrow living room windows.

"What's going on with you? You sound stoned or something."

152

"I've been sick," Clay answered, impatient to play the message on the answering machine. "You said something about getting together. When did you want to do that?"

"Boyd and I thought we should all sit down with Mom this weekend. I think it's important we're all there so it's clear we know what she's doing to herself and that it needs to stop."

Clay remained silent, still staring at the flashing message light.

"Hello? Are you there?"

"I'm here," Clay answered.

"Did you hear what I said?"

"You want to do something this weekend?"

"Are you sure you're okay?"

"I'm fine. Can we wrap this up? I have something I need to do."

"Does Saturday work?"

"Saturday. Sure. That's fine."

"Can you be in front of Mom's place at one?"

"I think so."

"It's important we're all there, Clay. Especially you. Mom tends to listen to you."

That last comment made him laugh. Eva was not going to listen to anyone at this point. It did not matter who talked to her.

"Also, I don't want Mom to know we're coming. I don't want her to have time to clean up and pretend everything is fine."

After promising to keep the visit a secret, he hung up the phone. There followed a small hesitation before he pushed the play button on the answering machine. Even as the machine rewound the tape, he knew the detective had left the message for the simple fact Clay had no interest in talking to him.

"Give me a call, Clay," came the detective's gruff message. "We've got a bit of an issue going on here, and I need to talk to you."

Just the sound of the man's voice was enough to unsettle the last of Clay's moderately stable thoughts. It took some time before he finally dialed the detective's number. He reminded himself to relax. The detective was only having an issue with some bullshit related to the Nichols brothers. The detective's work number went to voicemail. Clay left a message. The uncertainty of the detective's message along with Margaret's phone call weighed down all the other stress he felt, making it hard to figure out what to do next.

3:49 a.m.

The living room sat in a near-complete darkness. The wind howled outside, rattling the small apartment windows. The power had been out for some time. Clay had just finished a phone call with Melissa. The storm blowing through the region had proved more violent than forecasted, and she needed him to come to the newsroom to help catalog the damage.

With his eyes adjusted to the lightless space, he could see outlines of some of the stationary forms around him. The coffee table. The television. But not much else. This lack of sight made him uneasy, as if someone else were lurking in the claustrophobic space of the apartment. He kept looking to his side and behind him, expecting something to be there. It made it hard to concentrate. In truth, Melissa's call could not have come at a better time since it would give him a reason to get out of the apartment.

When Melissa had called, he could hear a smile in her voice. She lived for these kinds of emergency-filled moments where the urgency of a story pushed all other responsibilities to the side.

"We're getting reports from all over the area about trees falling on houses and a host of injuries," she had said.

"Who else is coming in?"

"You're it, so far. I'm going to try a couple of others, but since you're the deepest in my doghouse you're definitely helping out on this."

"Where should I start?"

"Come to the newsroom. We're still getting things organized."

"Do you have power?"

"Nope. At this point the scanner is running on batteries and we have flashlights, pencils, and paper."

"I'll be there in about fifteen minutes."

"Make it ten!"

Despite the directive to hurry, Clay continued to sit on the couch and listen to the wail of the wind and the rain trundling down like pebbles hitting the sidewalk. He looked to his left. The incoherent mixing of sounds created the sensation of someone babbling into his ear. The room's silhouetted shadows shifted, like a gust of wind had blown through. He could smell the rain now, the room filling with an organic-scented mixture of earth and moisture.

Clay closed his eyes. His hands shook, and he felt himself begin to rock back and forth. The surface of his skin tingled, and the sound of voices started to come from behind him. He opened his eyes and turned, but only found a darkness that appeared to stretch forever.

He stood and flipped on the nearest light switch; everything remained pitch black. He moved from the living room to the bedroom where the darkness grew so complete he could no longer tell whether his eyes were open or closed. No shadows. No shapes. Only sound. The smell of the rain. If he could just disappear into that darkness for a while. To have enough time to figure out what he was doing. But there was no more time to think. There was nowhere to go and hide.

Afternoon

L ights glowed from several windows in the apartment building. At least he would have power, he thought. The illumination, however, did nothing to ease Clay's nerves at returning home. A patchwork of lights dotted the city and surrounding suburbs as power slowly returned to the area. The windstorm had dissipated for the most part, but a hard rain still fell.

Clay had spent the last twenty-four hours reporting on the storm; exhaustion hung on every muscle in his body. He would have remained at work, though, if Melissa had not ordered him to leave. Work was preferable to this. Preferable to a place filled with ghosts and unavoidable sleep. He did not want to sleep, did not want to dream, did not want to remember all the terrible things he had done.

A shock of static stung him as he unlocked the apartment door. Inside, several lights were already on. Standing in the small entryway, he listened for the sound of something other than the rain and distant traffic. But there was nothing. Setting the keys on the counter, he proceeded to turn on all the kitchen and living room lights as well as the lights in the bedroom, creating a pale-yellow luminescent glow. He took a seat on the couch, his hands clasped in tight fists on his lap. No shadows. Nothing discernable. Not with the lights cocked at different angles.

He fought the urge to lie down, to forget about the shadows, the sounds, the headaches, the muscle cramps.

His eyes drifted closed. By avoiding the bedroom, he had hoped to stay awake. That, however, was not going to happen as he listed to his left, his head coming to rest against the arm of the couch. Don't sleep, he thought. Please, get up, he thought, his muscles unwilling to act on this simple request. He needed to get up. It was too late, though. Exhaustion easily brushed aside his feeble attempt to move. He was asleep now, his head filling with phantasmal sounds, intensifying and growing louder like an approaching siren.

9:32 p.m.

The pulse of the bar's jukebox mixed with the clatter of voices to create an indecipherable wall of noise. Kiki watched the ghostly shapes swirling within the clouds of cigarette smoke; she felt the unsteady sway of her drunken body.

Each drink—and she had already lost count of the number of drinks—heightened this sense of instability. That was the idea, wasn't it? To reach a level of intoxication that obliterated all thought. To forget what had happened. To pretend there was nothing to forget. If she ended up slumped over a toilet throwing up, so be it. The moment, this moment, was about forgetting, separating herself from the man's weight that continued to press down on her chest, making it impossible to breathe, his sour breath polluting her senses. Her hands, even as she sat there, trembled despite her best efforts to force the fear from her mind. After the attack, while waiting for the police to arrive, Kiki had dialed Nana's number and listened to the discordant chimes that announced no one was going to answer. Despite the robotic voice reminding her the number was disconnected, Kiki had talked anyway, shading her voice in such a way as to make it sound like Nana; she spoke words of comfort, encouraging herself not to be afraid, to be strong.

Melanie bumped up against the table and set a shot of jaundice-colored tequila in front of Kiki, and then took a seat on the bench next to her. Julie, a friend of theirs from high school, sat on the other side of the table. The three women were situated in a booth in the back corner of the 5 Point Cafe, a bar located on a strip of no-man's land between Seattle Center and downtown. It was a place for cheap, strong drinks. On Saturday nights, the bar's already off-kilter axis wobbled even more, making things spin faster and crazier than was often safe.

The monorail, not far from the bar, glided two stories above the rainy streets like a pendulum marking great swaths of time as it shuttled glazed-eyed tourists between the Space Needle and Westlake Center.

Melanie said something.

"What?" Kiki yelled.

"Drink up!"

Melanie and Julie raised their shot glasses to the middle of the table. Kiki brought her own glass up. The other two women shouted something unintelligible, and the three downed the awful-tasting liquid, their faces twisting in a convulsion of pain despite their already-deep intoxication.

Since the attack, Kiki had stayed at Melanie's apartment. Not that she felt safe there. Or could relax. Even during the day, in the most brightly lit spaces, she remained tense, keeping alert to who was around and what type of activity was occurring nearby.

"You doing okay?" Melanie asked.

"I'm drunk," Kiki yelled back with a smile.

Julie leaned forward. "What?"

It had been more than a year since Kiki had seen Julie, a thin woman with curly brown hair and a surfeit of cheerful energy. Kiki was not sure how to feel about seeing her again after so much time. Maybe it was everything that had happened with Nana and the recent attack, but Julie felt like a stranger despite the fact that the two women had once been such good friends. That seemed a long time ago, though. And that sense of distance, on top of everything else, added another layer of tangled emotions to the evening.

"It's good to see you," Kiki responded.

Julie smiled. "I'm sorry about what's been going on. I wish you'd called me when your grandmother died."

Kiki waved the comment away. "It's fine. I'm fine. What about you? How are things in Bellevue?"

The alcohol from the last shot burned through Kiki's bloodstream, further scattering her thoughts as she attempted to listen to Julie's response, struggling to process the words and sounds into something that had meaning. This "girls' night out" was Melanie's idea. Kiki had tried to talk her out of it. The idea of being around so many people had made her more stressed out. Now, however, thoroughly drunk, she almost felt relaxed, grateful for the bar's swirling chaos of noise and distractions.

Even at the relatively early hour of nine-thirty, the 5 Point had grown uncomfortably crowded. People packed into the small area between the booths and the bar, making it difficult to get from one end of the space to the other without knocking into someone. This had already resulted in at least one fight. One of the addicts who huddled near the statue of Chief Seattle not far from the bar had come in to use the toilet and seemed unaware of the people he bumped into as he made his way to the bathroom in the back. The rain had soaked the man's clothes and made his long black hair appear stringy and thin. His skeletal hands shook and displayed burn scars from the glass pipe clutched tightly in his fist. He had a broad face. Brown skin. And at that point in the evening, Kiki felt only moderately buzzed and remained keenly aware of who was in the bar, doing quick threat evaluations of each person. She had watched this man enter and disappear into the men's bathroom.

When he reemerged, she tracked him again, more out of curiosity than fear, as he pushed his way back through the crowd. The roundness of his chin and his deep-set eyes resembled her own features, perhaps echoing some distant genetic connection. The man had a lost quality about him as well. Something beyond blood and genetics. And as her thoughts drifted at the random possibilities, the junkie knocked into a man with geometric tattoos crisscrossing his arms. This, unknown to the addict, was the second time someone had bumped into the man and spilled his amber-colored beer onto his tight, black t-shirt. The man cursed and shoved the junkie in the back, sending the thin man sprawling to the floor. When the addict regained his feet, he spat in the direction of the other man's face and let loose a string of obscenities that produced more pushing. The junkie fell to the floor again, and the tattooed man kicked him in his soft, drug-sickened belly, the man's blunt-toed cowboy boot disappearing into the addict's stomach as though his body were liquid and not flesh and blood like the rest of the bar's patrons.

Without thought, Kiki had stood up and moved in the direction of the fight with some absurd idea of helping the man on the floor. She didn't get far, though, before the 5 Point's bouncer plowed through the crowd and grabbed the Indian by the collar and dragged him outside. Only the Indian, though. The tattooed man received an apology from the bartender and a fresh beer.

Julie shouted something, disrupting Kiki's thoughts. "…some kind of genealogy…"

Kiki shook her head no and pretended the question had focused on whether she was dating or not. "I'm not seeing anyone right now. How about you?" she asked, hoping to frustrate Julie's inquiry. She didn't want to talk about the family research. The attack. Or Nana's death. Didn't want to think about any of it even though she seemed unable to focus on anything else.

As Julie talked, Kiki's thoughts drifted to the newspaper clippings she had seen in the basement of the

Pioneer Square building. The brittle, yellowed newspapers had smelled of mildew and dust. The articles had spanned a period between 1875 and 1876 and centered on the murder of a Duwamish woman and the subsequent trial of the white man accused of the crime. The articles listed the man's name as Rueben Furth. The same name Kiki had found on the microfilm at the library a week before. Even now, it seemed hard to believe. The coincidence. When she first spotted the man's name among those old articles, she convinced herself she had misremembered the name, and so she didn't ask the woman who owned the building any questions. Kiki simply wrote down the date of each article with the intention of going to the library the next day to get her own copies. Later that night, a man broke into her apartment and attacked her, eliminating the urgency to find those articles.

She had finally made the trip to the downtown library that morning where she not only located the articles from the Pioneer Square building, but she also found a new article stating the murdered woman had had a child with the white man. None of the other articles had mentioned a child. At first, she wondered if it was a mistake; but when she tracked ahead on the microfilm machine, she soon found other newspapers that mentioned the child. Kiki read and reread each article as if expecting the words to somehow change. If this was the family connection she had been looking for, that Nana had been looking for, then the child mentioned in these newspapers was Kiki's ancestor. And if that was true, then the man named Rueben Furth had murdered her ancestral grandmother. This changed things. It felt like it changed everything. When she returned from the library, she had called the owner of the Pioneer Square building to find out what the woman knew about all of this but only managed to get her answering machine.

Kiki felt more certain than ever that this new information somehow tied back to her grandmother's death. Not that she could make any sense of it. Why would someone murder an elderly woman over something that had happened more than a century ago? What was the point? Or perhaps there was no point. And that felt as true as any of it. It made her sick to think about and made her feel even less safe, as if anything were possible now.

A gravelly voice emerged from the jukebox and sang about bad posture and laxatives. Pennyroyal tea. Kiki listened to the words as the world wobbled and spun, tried to get the music to fill her head and push out the confusion, fear, and anger that permeated every inch of her thoughts.

Julie and Melanie were leaning forward and talking to each other. Julie was saying something about a boy she was seeing, or someone she had seen. Melanie seemed to know the guy and was laughing. Maybe it was someone from high school because Melanie turned to Kiki and said a name like she should know the person. Kiki nodded as if she understood who they were talking about so as not to interrupt the flow of the conversation.

Her attention drifted upwards to the giant moose head that loomed above, a colorful array of bras dangling from its broad antlers and nose: blues and purples and whites and blacks and reds. A ridiculous rainbow of silk and lace. For the first time in days, she felt herself laugh. A real laugh. That poor fucking moose, she thought. From living in the fresh mountain air among beautiful cedar trees to being shot, stuffed, and mounted on a wall in a smoky bar with women's undergarments dangling from its face. She wondered if the women had come to the 5 Point expecting to throw their bras up there, or if it had happened in a fit of drunken spontaneity. She couldn't imagine a level of intoxication that would allow her to do something like that. It embarrassed her to even consider drawing that much attention to herself.

In the back corner of the bar, a black and white monitor alternated among three security cameras located in the Laundromat next door. The first view showed the lines of washers up against the wall in the main area. A short, heavy-set Latino woman worked to transfer laundry from one of the washers to a metal wire basket on wheels. White, rectangular folding tables went down the center of the room. A green, metal laundry detergent dispenser hung on the wall in the corner by the front door. The next scene displayed an area of the Laundromat where giant dryers formed a perfectly symmetrical line of Os. The third shot took in a small nook at the back where two dryers sat unused. There was something comforting about the quiet solitude of the Laundromat and its contrast to the overcrowded and impossibly loud environment of the bar.

A young boy and girl appeared asleep on a set of chairs a few feet from the woman doing laundry. The boy looked around eight years old and the girl five. Kiki had a hard time guessing the woman's age, however. Her movements were slow; her shoulders slumped forward. She could have been anywhere from twenty-eight to forty-eight. Kiki recognized the signs of exhaustion. It reminded her of how Nana looked after working a ten-hour shift at Harborview as a nurse's assistant and then coming home to cook and take care of her.

Kiki motioned for Melanie to scoot out. She needed to move. To get up and distract herself before she got caught up thinking about her grandmother. The goal of the night had been to avoid any kind of sad thoughts. She needed to find something else to focus on.

Free of the seat, Kiki bumped into several people as she pushed her way to the bar. If she got drunk enough, she reasoned, she might simply pass out once she reached Melanie's apartment and avoid any more thoughts about murdered Indians. No more nightmares. No more anything.

At the bar, she squeezed between two men seated on barstools and unsuccessfully tried to get the bartender's attention. A foot away sat the condiment tray with its neon-green limes, unnaturally red maraschino cherries, yellow lemons, and pickled green olives. She found herself craving something sour and took a quarter slice of lime from the tray; the bitter citric acid of the lime juice exploded across her taste buds as she bit into it, sending a quiver of delight through her body.

From behind, a surge of people pushed her tight against the bar. The noise rose and blurred into an incoherent vibration. She turned, afraid another fight had broken out. But there was no fight. Just too many bodies crowding into too small a space. The floor shifted beneath her. The cigarette smoke from the two men next to her accelerated a feeling of nauseated unbalance. Perhaps if she went outside. Got some fresh air. But then the bartender appeared, and she heard herself order three more shots, easily dismissing the internal voice that warned her not to drink anymore.

With the drinks precariously balanced between the fingers of her two hands, she carefully negotiated her way back through the crowd. It wasn't until she reached the table that she saw the three guys sitting with Melanie and Julie. In that instant, she wanted to turn around and leave. This wasn't why she had gone out tonight, to engage in empty small talk with people she didn't know, people she wanted nothing to do with. But Melanie had already seen her and taken the drinks, directing Kiki to sit next to a thin man with wisps of facial hair on his upper lip and chin.

A shot glass found its way to Kiki's hand and the male interlopers chanted their juvenile encouragement, a sound that reignited her anger and intensified her wish to go home. The one sitting next to her grabbed her arm and said something that got swallowed up by the noise. She pushed his hand away. He laughed. This provoked her anger; she failed to see the humor in her pushing his hand away. Or was he just laughing at her?

The man leaned closer and put his lips next to her ear. "I'm just offering to get you another drink," he said. His breath smelled of beer and cigarettes. "I'm not going to hurt you."

Kiki leaned away and moved to the outer edge of the booth. She wanted to leave, to go home to her own apartment and not be afraid. The boys sitting with Melanie and Julie lit cigarettes, sending a fresh bloom of smoke into the air. The surrounding bar patrons shouted and yelled, the volume escalating with the room's intoxication, making it impossible to concentrate on any single thought or movement.

"What?" Kiki asked. But no one had said anything to her. Melanie and Julie were wrapped up in conversations with the other two guys.

"Let me get you a drink!" the man next to her shouted.

"I'm fine."

"I'm going to bring a drink… Might as well buy you something…"

Kiki tried to get Melanie's attention. She wanted to go, catch a cab back to Melanie's apartment, and watch television until Melanie returned. She didn't have to sleep. She could stay up and wait.

"I'll bring you another shot," the boy yelled into her ear. He then made her stand up as he collected orders from the others at the table.

"Melanie? Melanie! I'm going to go back to the apartment," Kiki said, still standing.

Melanie looked up and said, "What?"

"I'm going to go back to the apartment!"

Melanie seemed to think about this for a moment and then nodded as if she understood. The bar noise, however, was so loud and everyone so drunk that it was almost impossible to understand anything at all.

The black-and-white monitor in the corner continued to switch among the different cameras. Nothing had changed. The Latino woman and her two kids were still there. The rest of the place sat empty. Kiki slowly started to wade through the human congestion that obstructed the exit. She felt certain that once she reached Melanie's apartment she would have to throw up. Things were spinning uncomfortably fast now.

Outside, fresh air filled her lungs and the bar music quieted to a muffled thump. A misty rain fell, throwing a thin veil around the hard edges of the charcoal-gray night. Sheltered by the bar's canvas awning, Kiki closed her eyes. Her body swayed. The reassuring rhythm of the rain slowed and soothed her emotionally twisted thoughts. She listened to the nearby traffic traveling along Denny Way as the cars hydroplaned through large puddles and sent up geysers.

Opening her eyes, she watched her breath drift into the cool, rainy night. A monorail car glided across the nearby track. The bronze statue of Chief Seattle stood a few yards away, barely visible in the dark night. The statue's upraised arm and open hand appeared like a plea to the rain and traffic to slow down as the world seemed on the verge of spinning out of control from the excessive noise and pollution. The light. Everything moving at such an impossible pace.

Kiki stumbled into the rain and found herself wandering over to the Laundromat. As the door closed behind her, the quiet hum of a drier replaced the mechanical acceleration of cars. The space was warm and smelled of detergent and fabric softener. The Hispanic woman sat in a chair, the two children resting their heads on her lap, her hand gently stroking her daughter's smooth black hair.

The alcohol made Kiki's movements feel like floating. She headed to the isolated driers in the back corner; the silver and black security camera looked like a laser from some low-budget science fiction movie. A red light at the top of the camera came on, stayed lit for several seconds, and then went off. She liked the quiet of this space. The sense of being alone, invisible. She wondered if Melanie would look up and see her as she stood there and watched the red light go on and off several more times, her body swaying to an unseen force. She then walked back towards the front, the echo of her footsteps sounding distant and strange.

At the Laundromat's large front window, a figure stood peering in, his hands cupped around his eyes as he leaned against the glass; the man's outline appeared to blend with the night's ambient half-light. A hood shadowed the upper half of his face, leaving only the tip of his nose and jawline visible. That was enough, though, to make Kiki stop. The thin frame and angular facial features resembled those of the man she had seen on the sidewalk outside her apartment.

The figure stepped back from the window. A tangled mix of fear and anger surged inside of her, the intense intoxication of the alcohol making it difficult to separate the two conflicting emotions. Her chest hurt, as if something heavy had suddenly pressed down on it.

The man turned and began to walk away. With little thought, Kiki moved to the front of the Laundromat and pushed open the door, stepping back out into the rain; adrenaline fought with the alcohol to clear her head and get her to understand what she was about to do. The dark, rainy night made it hard to see. She shouted the word "stop" as the shadowed figure, now moving at a slow jog, disappeared into the alley across the street. With only a slight hesitation, she chased after him.

Melanie had noted Kiki's absence, but the alcohol and flirting had sidetracked her concerns. It was not until someone suggested the group move to another bar that she started to look for her.

The first place she checked was the bathroom. She then pushed her way through the packed bar to see if Kiki might have gone to the diner side of the 5 Point. With no sign of her there, Melanie stepped outside. The rain was a downpour now.

"Kiki?" Melanie shouted into the empty night air. To keep steady, she put a hand against the building's brick wall. A nearby traffic light changed from red to green. The waiting cars accelerated.

"Kiki!"

Melanie stood there, uncertain of what to do next, the city's white noise pulsing in the background.

Melanie went to the payphone next to the entrance and dialed her own number. The phone rang five times before the answering machine clicked on. "Kiki, this is Melanie. What the hell happened to you? I'm on my way back so don't go anywhere."

"I'm sure she's fine," Julie said, coming up next Melanie.

Melanie looked back out at the rain. The rumble of the surrounding city noise continued its unending rise and fall.

Afternoon

W hat's with the secrecy? Clay asked, buckling himself into the passenger seat of the unmarked patrol car.

"No secrecy," the detective answered. "I was under the impression you were still doing a story on the murder of the Nichols brothers."

"I am. But why wouldn't you tell me where we were going when I talked to you on the phone?"

"Does it matter?"

"Yes, it matters!" Clay's voice rose more than he had intended, and he immediately attempted to calm himself down, to ignore the anxiety the detective's call had caused. "You've offered up enough unpleasant surprises to make me want to know what we're doing beforehand."

"Relax. No surprises. Just need to track down Justin."

"You still haven't heard anything from him?"

"Nope. His mom is avoiding my calls now, so we're going to check there first."

"His mom?"

"Yes," the detective laughed, "the kid has to live somewhere. He puts on gangster airs but he's nothing more than a momma's boy. By the way, how are you doing? You look as thin and pale as ever."

"And you still look like you could lose forty pounds," Clay said and looked out the passenger window. He did not like this. Being here with the detective. When the detective had called, Clay's immediate thought was to get out of it, to make up an excuse and not go. But that would not have looked right. He wanted things to look right. So he had agreed. And now he felt a desperate need to get as far away from the detective as possible.

"I do have one quick side errand to make on a missing person case before we start the hunt for Redman. I hope that won't qualify as an 'unpleasant surprise.'"

"A missing person case? Isn't that a bit beneath your pay grade?"

"The woman's been gone since Saturday, and a few days before that she had been attacked in her apartment so I'm working on the assumption that it's a homicide and we just haven't found the body."

A crackle of voices played over the car's police radio.

"Where's the apartment?"

"Capitol Hill."

Clay fell quiet. An unpleasant set of images flashed through his head. He tried to focus on something outside of the car. He clenched his perspiring hands and then rubbed them against his khaki slacks. The detective slowed and stopped at a red light and turned on the blinker to take a left onto Pike Street.

"Where on Capitol Hill are we going?"

"It's just a few blocks east of Broadway."

"Would you mind doing that later?" Clay asked. "I've got to get back to work soon and finish a story for tomorrow's paper. I don't have a lot of time right now."

The detective gave Clay an annoyed look. "This isn't going to take but a few minutes. You don't even have to get out of the car."

"It's not that. Never mind. Just make it quick, please." Clay considered asking the detective to pull over and let him get out. This was a mistake. Being here with him. It would have been better to go home and sleep. To dream. To pretend none of this was happening. "With the storm last week, I forgot to follow up on the message you left."

"Last week?"

"On my home phone. I think you left it right after the storm. You said we needed to talk, but you didn't mention what it was about?"

"Oh, right. That wasn't last week, though. I left that message Sunday."

The confusion with the days made Clay pause for a moment. "Okay, Sunday. What did you want?" And as he thought about it, he wasn't entirely sure what day of the week today was.

"I was calling about that metal box we dug up. There were a couple of pieces in there I wanted to look at again."

"Why?"

"Because that's what I do, Clay. I'm a detective. I look at things. I ask questions. I investigate. But we can talk about that later. It's nothing urgent."

This casual dismissal, however, only distressed Clay more. "If it's nothing urgent, then explain to me why you need to look at any of that stuff at all. I've already explained the things in the box were from my family. So, please, stop trying to convince yourself I'm some sort of thief."

The detective's eyes remained focused on the road, seemingly unfazed by the challenging tone of Clay's voice. "If you say none of those items are stolen, great. Then what's the problem with me looking at a couple of them again?"

"Because it feels like you don't believe me. And I don't like that. I also don't like all this poking around bullshit."

"Poking around?" the detective laughed. "You need to relax, my friend. I just want to look at a couple of pieces of jewelry, not indict you."

It would be better to let this go. The more he talked, the more likely he was to say something inappropriate. The need to defend and justify himself, however, overwhelmed his sense of caution. "What is it you think I'm guilty of?"

173

"I don't know, you tell me," the detective said.

Clay shook his head and looked away. There was no reason to continue the back and forth. The detective only wanted to goad him into some sort of confession. Clay needed to keep his mouth shut and put this whole fucking mess behind him.

"What about the sleepwalking? You still sticking to that story?"

Clay ignored the question, his eyes focused on the passing gray landscape.

"Come on, I can't be the first person to call bullshit on this. Don't get me wrong, you were definitely out of it that night at Volunteer Park. But you seemed more drunk than asleep. You know what I mean?"

The interrogating tone of the detective's voice tightened the knots in Clay's stomach. "No, I don't know what you mean. And, honestly, I really don't care if you believe me or not. You're welcome to your own opinion."

The detective gave a curt nod. "I appreciate that. But I've gotten off track. The metal box. What I wanted to look at was the ring with the Masonic symbol on it. I came across a description of something that sounded similar. In fact, it was part of this missing person case. I just wanted to see it. That's all. I'm not trying to accuse you of anything. So relax."

Relax? The thought made Clay laugh. His ability to relax had disappeared months ago, if it had ever existed at all.

The detective parked in the loading zone in front of a beige-brick, Art-Deco apartment building.

"Are you staying in the car?" the detective asked as he got out.

Clay hesitated. "No, I'll come."

The outside air was calm, the temperature somewhere in the mid-50s. At the secured entrance, the detective pushed the buzzer for an apartment on the fourth floor. There was no answer. The detective buzzed again and waited.

"No one home," Clay said. "Can we go now?" It was difficult to hear, to concentrate on something other than the blood pulsing in his ears.

"Nope. We're going in."

Just then, someone exited the building. The detective caught the heavy entrance door before it closed and they both entered. Clay followed the detective up the creaky stairs to the top floor. At apartment 406, the detective gave a loud, solid knock on the door. Clay had to stop himself from rubbing his hands together. It made him look anxious, and he knew the detective would notice that. No one came to the door. Clay strained to hear any kind of noise or movement coming from inside the apartment. Nothing. The entire floor remained quiet.

Clay was about to turn and walk back to the stairs when the detective took out a thin piece of plastic about the size of a credit card.

"It doesn't matter what lock you put on these old doors. When there's this much space between the frame and the door anyone can get in without a key," the detective said and then slipped the card into the gap.

"Don't you need a superintendent or someone to let you in? Or have a warrant, maybe?"

"Probably," the detective said with a shrug as he popped the lock and opened the door.

Clay took a step back. He did not want to be there. Did not want to enter. Too many things could go wrong. Too many things had already gone wrong.

"Seattle Police Department!" the detective called out through the open door. "Anyone here?"

It had the feel of a trap. Like the detective was trying to catch him off guard.

After announcing himself again, the detective gave Clay an impatient wave to come into the apartment. "Get

175

in here and shut the door behind you. And don't touch anything."

Unable to think of an excuse to avoid entering, he reluctantly walked in and carefully closed the door. The apartment's hardwood floors had deep scuffmarks. The kitchen looked as if the last renovation had taken place in the 1970s with its round-cornered refrigerator and yellow and white linoleum floor.

The detective worked his way across the living room and into the bedroom.

Stacks of books and papers covered the dining room table. Clay stepped over to the table and glanced at one of the piles. At the top of the stack were photocopies from an old hand-written journal. The top page was an entry from June 20:

> ...Mama's terribly sick, too. She could do nothing but sob and plead for Papa to stop when he hit me...

Seeing the detective still searching the bedroom, Clay grabbed the pages of the journal off the top of the stack and hid them in an inside pocket of his jacket. He then stepped away from the table, his nerves and chest tight, moving over to the bank of windows that looked down on the street.

"Doesn't look like anyone's been in this place since the woman went missing on Saturday," the detective said, going through the refrigerator and several cupboards. "A friend of the missing woman keeps calling the department and asking for updates. She doesn't want to accept my explanation that her friend might have taken an unannounced vacation. She's convinced this other woman was kidnapped or something."

Clay nodded. He looked over at the sidewalk across the street, at the tree there, the streetlight off to the right.

"Come on. I'm done. I needed to see if the woman had been back here. She hasn't. We can go look for James now."

"Good." The tone of Clay's voice, just in that single word, sounded uneasy even to him.

Going down the stairs, he trailed several steps behind, unwilling to get caught up in a conversation with the detective.

Back in the car, the detective sat there for some time, a heavy silence filling the space. "So what do you think?" he asked.

"About what?"

"About the woman that lives in the apartment?"

Clay stared at his hands and tried to keep his facial features as relaxed as possible. "I have no idea," he said. "I hope she's okay, I guess." The pages of the journal in his jacket pocket crinkled as he moved. He wondered if he had gotten all of it. He had only taken the sheets on top. There had been other loose papers further down the stack. And as he sat there, he knew he would have to return to make sure he had recovered the entire journal. He could not risk the detective finding any of it.

"...missing on Saturday...a group drinking...her friend's apartment..."

"I'm sorry," Clay interrupted, "I missed that. What were you saying?"

"It's nothing. You should see a doctor, Clay. You have an unhealthy look about you."

"And you should mind your own business," he snapped back. He tried not to dwell on the fact that the detective had brought him here. It did not matter. The detective did not know anything. There was nothing to be upset or worried about.

The detective started up the car. "You need to check your attitude, paperboy. You hear me? I'm doing these little fieldtrips as a favor to you. Remember that. In fact, I'll go ahead and track James down on my own."

177

"Right," Clay responded. He needed to go home. His head ached, and he felt sick to his stomach. "You can drop me back at my apartment."

Evening

What happened to you, Clay? The anger in his sister's voice caught him off guard.

He had answered the phone without giving much consideration to who it might be. It did not matter. He wanted to hear another person's voice, something to offset the clatter of his own thoughts.

"Happened?" The question confused him. What had he forgotten?

"Mom's! The three of us were meeting with Mom on Saturday! You, Boyd, and me. I talked to you about this last week. Do you remember us talking about that?"

"I remember," Clay answered. "I'm sorry about that. Something came up." The tone of his sister's voice. The accusatory questions. It reminded him of the earlier confrontation with the detective and his endless, looping interrogation.

"You couldn't call me and let me know you wouldn't be there? For Christ's sake, I left a dozen messages for you on Saturday."

The red light on the answering machine blinked, just as it had done for the last few days. "My answering machine hasn't been working."

"We were counting on you…"

Clay let his head drop and angled the phone away from his ear, debating whether to hang up or not. His thoughts wandered back to the woman's apartment and the stacks of research material on the table. The scratches on the wood floors. The view from the window. "What do you want me to do?" he said, bringing the phone back and cutting his sister off mid-sentence. "I'm sorry. I apologize. That's the best I can do right now."

"It would have helped to have you there."

"I don't know about that. Were you and Boyd able to talk to her?"

Mary gave a terse laugh and her voice took on a slightly more relaxed tone. "A little. She wanted to throw us out the minute we showed up."

"Did you ask her about the drinking?"

"Of course we did. She denied there was a problem," Mary said. "She claimed the mess you and I saw was a result of her being ill and had nothing to do with alcohol and more to do with the cold medication she had taken."

If Clay had not been so distracted, he might have laughed at Eva's clumsy excuse. But the words barely registered. Mary continued to talk, the drone of her voice slipping into the background. There was too much to think about. Too many details to work out. Clay lost track of time. He had stopped by Eva's a few days ago. The visit had been to pick up the family papers from the Pioneer Square building. He could not remember if Eva had mentioned anything about the encounter with Margaret and Boyd. Not that he would have remembered. The purpose of the visit was to get the boxes. Nothing else. He had not cared or thought about anything else.

A chaotic mix of papers, photos, newspaper clippings, and other ephemera from those boxes covered the coffee table and spilled across the surrounding floor.

"…really worried about you."

"What? About me? Why?" Clay asked, his attention momentarily drawn back into the conversation.

"She thinks you're having some sort of mental break."

"Oh." That was where he stopped listening again; there was no energy to debate the issue; in fact, he agreed with it. The idea of a mental break seemed almost comforting, as if, at one point, he had possessed a normal set of thoughts and emotions. Not long after this exchange, he hung up the phone.

He stood and went into the bathroom and took a benzodiazepine from the prescription bottle. This was the second dose in the last hour or so. He returned to the couch and resumed looking through the loosely organized piles, his hands trembling, as if handling something toxic, as he sorted through the material.

At the center of the coffee table sat an old newspaper article dated March 29, 1876. The yellowed and faded sheet was nearly unreadable. Pieces of the brittle newsprint had fallen off when he first took it out of the box. The article covered a murder trial. The name of the accused was difficult to make out. Difficult, but not impossible. Clay knew the name well: Reuben, his great-great-great grandfather. The article was not a complete surprise. He had hoped nothing like this would be in the boxes. But he had expected it.

He picked up the article and let it crumble in his hand, small pieces of antique paper raining down and littering the carpet. All of this needed to go, he thought, looking across the mess spread out in front of him. None of it should have been kept. It only invited curiosity and the dredging up of a past that needed to remain buried.

Clay stood. The quiet of the apartment, the heat and constraint of the space, made it difficult to think. He walked across the documents on the floor on his way to the kitchen to grab his keys off the counter.

Outside, the world vibrated with the rumble of traffic and gray light. There had been a picture at the missing woman's apartment: a little girl sitting on her grandmother's lap. The older woman was laughing, and the young girl had a playful smile on her face. The image refused to leave him alone, blistering his brain like a third-degree burn. He wanted to forget; had tried to forget.

Moving at a near jog, he headed up Queen Anne Avenue. The nighttime sky glowed with the reflected city lights. No stars. No rain. The benzos had done nothing to calm him down. The opposite felt true. Like the drugs were making him more frantic. More tense. The thumping of blood pulsed in his ears, competing with the chorus of city noises. The watch on his wrist counted out time. The secondhand moved around the white circular watch face; each tick of time felt like the closing moments of a race he had already lost.

Morning

Clay stood in front of the partially opened living room window that looked out on Madison Avenue. He could hear his mom wrestling with the coffee pot. It was early. Not too early. A few minutes past eleven. The window was open enough to let in small gusts of wind that made the thin white curtains dance in a billowing waltz of turns and twists.

"What did you say?" she asked.

"A murder." His voice barely registered above a mumble, though.

"I can't hear you, Clay."

"I said I found things about a murder in one of the boxes you gave me. Do you know anything about it?"

"A murder?" The sound of drawers opening and closing masked the rest of her response. "…all."

Looking out across the leafless trees and crisscrossing power lines, he wished he had been able to sleep. Maybe he would ask Eva if he could take a short nap here. Lie down on the couch and have her watch him to make sure he did not go anywhere. Maybe.

The warm smell of brewing coffee filtered into the room. "Would you pour me a cup, too?" he asked.

"Sure. Shouldn't you be at work?"

"I'm going in late to cover an evening meeting." The mixture of lies and truth came out with an effortless ease. He kept his eyes focused on the trees outside, wondering how much longer he could go on like this. No sleep. The constant fight against the unending rush of unsettled thoughts and disturbed mental images. The things he had done.

When his mom came in with the coffee, he returned to the couch. She handed him one of the cups and then took a seat in a nearby chair. Eva had already been awake when he rang the intercom. She did not sound or look hung over. The apartment was picked up. No unpleasant odors.

"Now what is this about a murder?"

The first sip of coffee burnt the roof of Clay's mouth. "There were newspaper clippings in the boxes from the Pioneer Square building."

"And?"

"And there was a group of articles from the 1870s talking about a man named Rueben being on trial for murder."

"Really?"

"Yes."

"What was the last name?"

"Petersen."

The room went quiet for a few moments. "I don't remember anyone ever mentioning a murder. If you're right about the name in the article, it's the same as your great-great-great grandfather. Who was he accused of murdering?"

"His wife."

"No, that can't be right. Must be a different man. If I remember correctly, his wife, your great-great-great grandmother, died on the trip out here from Illinois. In fact, I think one of his daughters died, too. Other than himself, the only survivor was his daughter Margaret, your great-great grandmother. She's the one who rebuilt the Pioneer Square building after the 1889 fire. And she collected most of the stuff in those boxes."

Clay gave a tired grunt. "I don't know. The articles also mentioned that Rueben and the murdered woman had a young daughter. Her name wasn't Margaret, though."

"It has to be a mistake."

"Why is it in those boxes?"

"I don't know, Clay. Maybe as a joke because the man shared the same name as her father. Besides, I would have heard about a second marriage and other children. Not to mention a murder."

Clay scratched at a scab on the top of his hand. Dark lines of dirt remained wedged beneath his fingernails. "I'm just telling you what I found."

"What was the woman's name? The one who was murdered?"

"I don't remember," he lied. He took off a gold ring from his index finger. "I also found this," he said. He put it on the coffee table. "I wasn't sure if you wanted it or not."

Eva picked up the ring. "Your father's wedding band?" she laughed. "You found this in one of the boxes?"

"No, it was in some other stuff I had."

"How in the world did you end up with this?"

Clay shrugged and looked at his watch. It was eleven thirty-five.

"This was such a long time ago," she said with the hint of a smile. "It's an interesting relic. But I don't want it." She handed it back to him. "Try your father. Or better yet, melt it down and sell the gold."

Clay absently turned the ring over with his fingers. The ostensible reason for coming here had been to ask about the murder. As if he still had questions. But it no longer felt important. There were other errands to run, and he needed to think about leaving soon.

"Did the articles say anything more about the crime?"

"Not really." He tried to force his mind away from thoughts of the murder.

"Are you all right?"

185

"I'm fine. Tired." That admission felt like the first honest thing he had said.

"Have you been sleepwalking?"

"No."

Clay stood and returned to the window.

"...see someone ..."

But he wasn't listening. His eyes searched the street below, half expecting to see the detective's car among those parked along the road. "I should get going," he mumbled. Brown and orange leaves littered the gray sidewalk. Through the thin pane of glass, he could feel the cool air pushing itself into the room; the smell of winter dampness filled his head like a narcotic.

"...make an appointment for you? I could go with you, Clay."

There was a note of concern in Eva's voice that caught him off guard. The idea of someone worrying about him felt foreign. He wanted to tell her to relax; she had no reason to worry. He was fine. Everything was going to be fine. But he failed to gather the necessary energy for the lie. Instead, he watched a gust of wind send the leaves skittering across the hard ground below. The smell of rain scented the air. An interlacing array of skeletal branches carved up the late morning sky. Each of these things offered a sense of the normal, a normal he wished he could feel. With a deep exhale, his breath spread a fog across the window like the sign of a passing ghost. Eva said something, but he missed most of it. "What was that?"

"I said you look sick. You don't look well," his mom repeated.

"I'm fighting a bit of the flu." She was right, though. He was not well. Pieces of himself had grown sick. A gangrenous type of infection. That was how it felt, at least. He moved away from the window and grabbed his jacket from the couch.

Eva stood. "When was the last time you ate? Or slept?"

Clay smiled. "It's all right. I'm fine."

"You don't look fine. Why don't you sit down and I'll make a couple of calls and see if someone can see you today? We'll go together."

He shook his head. "I'm not going to meet with anyone. I just came by to see how you were doing. That's all." And that, in part, felt true. He had not really come about the murder. That was simply one piece of the lie he had told himself to keep from thinking about the truth. No, he had made the visit to say goodbye. That was it. He needed to say goodbye. Nothing more.

"I know you and Mary and Boyd are worried about me," she said with an uncomfortable laugh. "And I know I didn't handle their visit very well. But I'm getting things back on track. Just give me some time. Okay? So let me help you. Let's get you better. I need you to be well, too."

"I'll give you a call in a day or two," he said. With that, he brushed past her and left.

Daytime

Kiki's breathing came in quick, arhythmical bursts. Tape covered her mouth. She lay on her back. Her eyes darted from side to side, vaguely recognizing the crudely framed walls, like those of a tree fort, that surrounded her. Cedar branches loomed overhead.

For a strange, surreal moment, she seemed to know this place. It didn't make any sense, though. Couldn't make any sense. How had she ended up at the treehouse in Nana's backyard? It felt like a trick. Another plot to further confuse her fevered mind.

She tried to move, but straps across her chest and waist made it impossible to even roll over. Zip ties bound her wrists, ankles, and knees. She struggled, again, against the restraints, her body convulsing from the confluence of cold and panic, hunger and thirst. A painful headache racked her head, and a baseball-sized lump bulged from the right side of her skull where her hair was stiff and crusted with what she assumed was blood.

A sick, sticky wetness saturated her pants. The smell of urine and excrement mixed with the scent of mildewed plywood and cedar sap. The skin between her legs and buttocks itched and burned.

Raw pressure ulcers lacerated her tailbone, ankles, and shoulders. Amongst all the other foul odors, she recognized the unmistakable smell of rotting tissue, a scent she knew from her work at the hospital. If untreated, these wounds would spread infection to her muscles and bones, to her heart and lungs, advancing until they killed her. She knew this. And she struggled again against the restraints as tears welled up and slid down the side of her face, making it impossible to see.

The singing of a nearby bird melded with the soft patter of rain.

She screamed. A muffled howl that issued from deep within her and continued for a long time even though the tape and surrounding tree branches dampened and swallowed up every note of sound.

Afternoon

The traffic light remained red. It stayed that way for an uncomfortably long time. A forest-green Subaru wagon idled next to Clay. The driver, a woman, was looking down at something. She had her black hair pulled into a ponytail; a small strand hung loose across her cheek. Her nose had an aquiline quality to it, her chin round and soft. He liked the way she looked. Pretty. Relaxed. Secure within the normal flow of the world. If things were different, maybe there would have been room for him to love someone like that.

The light turned green and he watched the car disappear up the street, his thoughts still wandering through all the different possibilities, preventing him from initially hearing the angry chorus of car horns that had started up behind him. It was not until the light turned yellow that he put the car in gear and accelerated. He should be at work. Had not been to work in several days. There were irate messages from Melissa on his answering machine. He had yet to call her back. There was not much of a reason to return her calls at this point.

Clay took a left on Pike Street. This followed the same route the detective had taken. Not that he was thinking about that. But he knew. He tried not to dwell on it even though that was all he had thought about. He should have gone earlier. It already felt like he was too late.

Up ahead, a light went from green to yellow to red. Clay slowed to a stop. Deep grooves creased the pale skin of his face. His unwashed hair was a mess. The tissue around his eyes was puffy and discolored. He felt unwell. Just as he looked. Cars cut across his field of vision, each one traveling with a linear clarity that felt unreal to him. How anyone could be possessed of such freedom. He wondered what that felt like. To move without the recognizable weight of history, the weight of so many thoughts and actions and crimes.

Here, a block from Broadway, young men and women dotted the sidewalks. Kiki could have been among them, walking to the grocery store or to a nearby coffee shop. Things should have been different. All it would have taken was for someone to do, to be something different. That was all. Nothing more than the simple will to change the very world itself. This thought made Clay smile. The world would be what the world was. And in this world, he reminded himself, he needed to buzz the apartment intercom before heading up. To be certain no one was there. Not her, of course. She would not be home. He did not need to worry about that. The detective troubled him, though, and the possibility of running into him. It would have been better to go at night. But he had a schedule now, and he needed to get all of this out of the way before he left.

As he drove past the apartment building, he saw no sign of the detective's car. He checked the rearview mirror, again, to make sure no one was following him. He circled the block and then parked about a hundred yards north of the address. Once out of the car, he crossed the street to approach the apartment building from the opposite side to get a more open view of the area.

The bare, spindly branches of the maple and oak trees along the sidewalk offered a spiderweb-like sense of concealment. He kept his focus on the windows of the fourth floor with some vague expectation of seeing shadows of movement in them. But there was nothing.

Above, soft, gray clouds hung uncomfortably low. No rain. Even so, the gray had drained all the color from the surrounding landscape. Across the street, Clay watched the building. His breathing came in short gasps that put him near to hyperventilating. Still no movement. No light. If he was going to go up there, he needed to go now. The longer he waited, the more people would notice him. He gave a quick glance up and down the sidewalk and then crossed the street. His hands had a wet, sticky feel to them.

At the building's entrance, his sense of exposure intensified. He looked up at the top floor. The overcast sky reflected off the glass, making it impossible to see anything else. He pressed the intercom for Kiki's apartment and waited. If the detective was there, Clay wondered if he would answer; it seemed a chance worth taking. After a few moments, he took out a card like the one the detective had used and quickly opened the aged security door.

Inside, the balustrade of the wide staircase swept upward like a menacing hand. The polished wood had a smooth, cool feel to it as Clay ascended the stairs, giving him something to focus on other than the anxious chatter of his thoughts that had grown angry and paranoid.

Reaching the top floor, the weight of his footsteps made the old floorboards creak and groan. If the detective was in the apartment, Clay wondered if the use of the intercom had acted as a warning; he leaned towards the door of apartment 406, closed his eyes, and listened. Anxiety knotted every muscle in his body. Nothing. No sounds. He grasped the brass doorknob, turned it, and pushed. To his surprise, the door opened. It should have been locked. He felt a rush of panic. Was someone there? He slowly stepped in, afraid to close the door all the way behind him. He listened.

"Hello?"

The apartment appeared much as it had on his visit with the detective. Very still. Very quiet. As if frozen. A red and black geometric patterned afghan rug spread across the middle of the living room, something he had not noticed before. A camel-colored couch sat at an angle to the wall where it had been pushed after being used as a wedge against the door. The stacks of books and papers on the dining-room table continued to stand like the silhouette of a distant skyline.

"Hello?" His voice barely rose above a murmur. He carefully closed the door and took a step towards the bedroom. "Kiki?"

The act of saying her name was nothing more than a gesture of self-delusion. She was not there. He knew that. He should have called out the detective's name. That was where the fear came from, imagining him hiding somewhere in that space, watching him, waiting for him to do or say something incriminating. The mere thought of this made it difficult to breathe, the thumping of his overworked heart filling his head.

He stood in the doorframe of the bedroom. All was dark. He did not want to turn on any lights. The dresser to the left and the queen-sized bed to the right were visible only as shadowed outlines. He stepped in and ran his hands across the bed, reassuring himself that it was empty.

Back in the living room, he returned to the cedar table and the piles of research material. This was what he had come for. He needed to figure out what to take with him to eliminate any connection between Kiki and himself. That included the remaining journal pages. But as he started to go through the material, he could tell something was wrong because there were no loose sheets in the stack that should have contained the rest of the journal. He checked the other stacks. There had been more pages. He felt certain of that. Right there, just under the first couple of books. Not anymore. Had he imagined it? The line between the physical world and his dreams had grown clouded and uncertain. He had felt so certain, though, about the need to return to the apartment and get those additional pages. Trying to push past the confusion, he resumed sorting through the material on the table, separating the books and loose papers into two piles: one that would stay and one he would take with him. After about fifteen minutes, he had assembled a small stack – mostly photocopies – that he would take home. He still had not found any additional pieces of the journal.

As he turned to leave, he noticed the blinking red light on the answering machine. The machine sat on an end table. He walked over and pushed the play button. A woman's voice emerged from the speaker. She sounded drunk, her words slurred and her voice louder than necessary. He could hear traffic in the background and the patter of rain against a fabric awning.

"Kiki?" the woman shouted. "Are you there? Pick up! I hope you went back to my apartment. If you get this, call me and leave a message. We're heading back."

The same woman left the next message as well. There was no background noise this time. She asked Kiki to call her. With only a small amount of tape left on the mini cassette, silence followed the next beep. Clay leaned forward to push the skip button but caught himself just as a man's voice spoke.

The first part of the message was indistinct and difficult to understand. Only the words "pick up" were clearly discernable. Even so, the voice itself made Clay's heart skip. A familiar voice. With a quick rewind, he replayed the message. At the last part of the message, it sounded like the man was saying the word "stop," or something like "I can't stop." It did not matter what the voice had said, however. The sound and tone of it was his. He had left the message. Without thinking, he popped the tape out of the machine and put it in his pocket. He looked around, half expecting the detective to step out from somewhere and start asking questions. He must have left the message in the last day or two. But why? He had no memory of the call. Or was this another trick of his exhausted mind? Had he only imagined it to be his voice? He considered putting the cassette back into the machine to play it, but the panic to leave overrode the urge.

With his mind scattering, he stepped to the window and scanned the parked cars along the street. Still no sign of the detective. A car alarm rang out somewhere. Clay's breathing quickened. The alarm's wail melded with the fluctuating sounds in his head.

He moved from the window. It was time to go. For a moment, he struggled to remember what he had touched since entering the apartment, what things he needed to wipe down; but he quickly dismissed the thought since wherever his fingerprints appeared could be linked to his visit with the detective.

He quietly opened the door and stepped out. Voices filtered up the staircase from somewhere in the building. He could not tell whether the individuals were coming up the stairs or going down. Clay remained frozen on the fourth-floor landing, fighting the compulsion to run. A few moments later, the front door of the apartment building opened and closed, taking the group of voices with it. The only sounds became the creak of stairs as he hustled his way out of the building.

Outside, the street felt narrow. Claustrophobic. He took a left and kept his head down as he walked. At the end of the block, he realized he had gone in the wrong direction. He turned back, the sense of fear growing, certain he would be spotted and remembered now. By the time he reached the car, he was at a full jog and out of breath. He struggled to get the car door open, balancing the stack of loose papers and books against the car as several pieces fell to the wet pavement before he finally wrestled the door open and threw the remaining material onto the passenger seat. He then quickly retrieved a book and some soaked photocopies from the ground.

Once inside the car, he fought to catch his breath, to calm himself down.

Evening

The noise of someone knocking on the apartment door barely registered. It should have startled Clay given his high state of mental distress. He had expected a visit from the detective at some point because of the multiple messages he had left on the answering machine. The loud, impatient knock made it clear he had arrived. Not that Clay wanted to see the detective. He had hoped to avoid him altogether; but Clay had failed to get his things ready to leave.

A jumbled mess of family papers, journal excerpts, and newspaper articles spread out in front of him to fill most of the open floor space in the living room. The rusting metal box from Volunteer Park sat on the coffee table. He had wanted to go over each piece of information to make sure he had not missed something. But it seemed the deeper he went into a specific detail, the more uncertainty and confusion he felt; for the last couple of hours, he had read and reread the same pioneer journal entries, each reading bringing up a new set of problems and questions.

> *A group of men from the wagon train carried Abby's body back to the north side of the river and buried her above the flood line. Hard to remember much of what happened. I know Abby and me was sitting next to Pa on the wagon seat as we rode into the water. We were about ten yards behind the lead wagon when we headed into the deepest section of river. Not long after that*

something from upstream hit us and pitched the wagon sideways.

Abby sat at the far edge of the wagon seat. I remember her thin body tumbling over the top of me as we went into the river.

I don't think we even had time to take a breath before hitting the freezing water.

Standing, he scooped up the items he remembered taking from the woman's apartment, dropped them in a nearby box, and folded the cardboard flaps over the top. The rest of the mess he left where it was.

Another series of loud knocks sounded at the door.

"You're alive," the detective said as Clay opened it. "You look like hell, but you're alive."

"What do you want?"

"I want to talk to you. All right if I come in?"

Clay hesitated, keeping the door only half-open and wishing he had taken more time to clean up. "I don't think that's a good idea right now. I'm not feeling well."

"Come on. I have some news I want to share. It'll take five minutes."

Clay could hear the lie in the detective's voice. There was not any pressing news to share. He only had questions he wanted to ask, which Clay had expected. "You have five minutes." Clay stepped aside and let the detective enter.

There was a numbness to Clay's movements and thoughts as he followed the man back to the living room. A small part of him welcomed this visit as it offered a rare distraction. But mostly he wanted him gone as quickly as possible. In the living room, he moved a stack of papers off a chair for the detective and then took a seat on the couch. Having all this material out in the open felt a bit like exposing a festering wound.

"Doing a little research?" the detective asked.

"Something like that."

The detective appeared to read something on the table. A newspaper article, maybe. "Wouldn't be a bad idea to air this place out," he said, looking up at Clay.

"Why are you here?"

"I wanted to give you an update on the body pulled from Portage Bay." The detective picked up the metal box of jewelry from the table and started to look through it.

"You couldn't do this over the phone?" Clay asked, intently watching him, wanting to get up and take the box away.

"I tried. I left you a couple of messages." The detective took out the Knights of Pythias ring from the box and made a close inspection of it.

"I've been busy. So what's this news that can't wait?" He should not have left the box out, he thought, angry with himself for being so careless. Should not have let the detective in at all. But within his flaring impatience came a hint of curiosity. How much did the detective suspect? Was there anything to be concerned about?

"We identified the boy pulled from the water as one of Justin's people."

"That's it? I thought you already knew that?"

"I recognized him, but I didn't have a name." The detective then held out the ring in his hand. "This is the piece I was asking you about. The one I wanted to see again. Any idea where it came from?"

The ring showed a three-colored shield of blue, yellow, and red. At the top of the shield was a knight's helmet flanked by pointed axes. "It's my great-great-great grandfather's. And I would appreciate it if you would put it back in the box and put the box back on the table."

"An interesting design," the detective said with a queer sort of smile, ignoring Clay's request.

"It's a fraternal order symbol. Like the Masons," Clay said.

"You wouldn't happen to have a beer, do you?"

"No. This is a quick visit, remember?"

"Just a beer. Besides, I'm doing you a favor by giving you this stuff on the body. None of it's been released yet." The detective smiled and then leaned back in the chair in a gesture that said he had no intention of leaving.

"One beer," Clay responded with undisguised irritation. He then went to the kitchen and grabbed two bottles from the refrigerator.

"We also got back the ballistics from the body and they match," the detective said as Clay handed him a beer.

He could not remember the last time he had eaten, so it did not take but a couple of drinks to feel a buzz. "The ballistics matched the bullets from the double homicide? The Nichols brothers?"

The detective took a long swallow of beer and resumed digging through the metal box. "Yep."

"So what does that mean?"

"Not sure. Could be a series of contract killings. Something to do with a gang feud or a fight over territory. You mind if I take this ring for a couple of days and have it photographed?"

Clay sat a little straighter. The detective had set the ring on the table along with several other pieces. "Yes, I do mind. And please tell me you don't still think this stuff is stolen?"

"The symbol matches a piece taken from the woman's apartment that you and I visited. I just need an example in order to do a little research. That's all. I'm not accusing you of anything."

"Okay," Clay said. He tried to make himself relax, or at least look relaxed. "Maybe later. I'm taking the box to my mom's this week to let her go through it. Maybe after that."

"Fair enough." The detective offered an innocent smile. "No law against asking."

Clay took a sip of beer and then wrapped the bottle in a tight grip. "Since you never got back to me on the original Portage Bay story, my editor wrote me up for failing to confirm the connection with those other murders." His voice had a bitter tenor to it. Not that he felt angry. He had a difficult time understanding what he felt. Several days had passed since he had last gone to work, several days since he had called Melissa and told her he was sick. She had left her own angry messages on the answering machine.

"Sorry, I just didn't have anything at that time. But now that I have the ballistics, I should be able to get you something."

Clay finished his beer and stood up. His balance was off. The alcohol had softened the edges a little, offering a hint of relaxation. "You want another beer?"

"Sure."

"What about Justin? Have you found him?" Clay asked from the kitchen.

"Not yet. Don't have a good feeling about it, either. The other thing I forgot to mention is we pulled fingerprints from the body in the ditch and actually matched them with a set at the Nichols' house."

Back in the living room, Clay handed another beer to the detective. "You still think the body in the ditch was the witness?"

"I do."

"What about the killer, then?" The questions came easy after so many years as a reporter. He could go on like this for hours despite how unsettled he felt.

"I've talked with a couple of LAPD gang-unit detectives to track down this Watts character, but so far it's been a dead end. Did you notice this?" the detective asked, holding up a plain gold ring. His voice sounded far away. "The ring has an inscription: Marge & John, 1935."

"Grandparents," Clay said.

"What's that?"

"Those are the names of my grandparents," he repeated. "The date is the year they were married. It's a wedding band."

"Got it." The detective dropped the ring into the box and sat back. "You like history?" His voice had an unwelcomed lecturing quality to it. Clay shrugged, suddenly growing less interested in the conversation. The detective, apparently, refused to get to the point of his visit. And so Clay's thoughts drifted back to the journal entries covering the Snake River crossing:

...hit river bottom and got dragged downstream. The water ran deep and fast. Managed to pull myself to the surface after getting tangled in a swarm of low-hanging willow branches. Someone grabbed my arms and dragged me ashore. There was all kinds of shouting upriver. I saw Pa struggle to unhitch the oxen as the upside-down wagon had wedged itself on some rocks. When I didn't see Abby, I started back towards the river, yelling her name. I must have been up to my waist in the water before I got pulled back...

"...bit of a history junky," the detective said. "Once I get hooked on a subject, I end up reading everything I can get my hands on. History always changes shape depending on who's telling the story."

"I thought you were here to talk about the Portage Bay murder. What does your love of history have to do with that?"

The detective laughed. "You are in a mood, aren't you?"

"It's been a difficult week. Make your point."

"History is everywhere," the detective said. "That's my point. For instance, did you know in 1856 an alliance of Indian tribes attacked this area's white settlers? In fact, it happened not far from your apartment here?"

Something about the direction of the conversation increased Clay's already considerable discomfort. "Is that right?"

The detective took a moment as if trying to pick a starting point for his story. "Have you heard of the Decatur?"

"It's a high school," Clay absently answered. He started to read the headline from a scrap of newspaper near his foot. The headline read *Man Cleared of Killing Indian Woman*.

"No," the detective said, a note of disappointment in his voice, "not the high school. This was the name of a nineteenth-century warship that singlehandedly turned back one of the largest Indian attacks in this city's history. You are aware tribes like the Duwamish used to live on the land around here before the settlers came?"

"Sure."

"Does that bother you?"

Clay took a drink of beer, still looking at the headline. "I don't know. Does it bother you?"

"A little bit."

Clay leaned down and picked up the article. "I appreciate the history lesson, but what does this have to do with anything?" Clay read the first couple of lines from the yellowed newspaper:

> *The man accused of killing an Indian woman was given a not guilty verdict. After the verdict, the man disavowed the child as his own, stating he wanted nothing to do with it...*

In the background, the detective spoke about cannon balls exploding in the forest and settlers fleeing into a blockhouse. Small pieces of the brittle newsprint cracked and splintered onto the coffee table. There were questions contained within that ancient ink he did not want to consider. The detective's voice went on about something that sounded vaguely familiar, familiar in a way that made Clay want to forget, to stop listening and think about something else.

203

"...the Indians would have overwhelmed the settlers," the detective said. "Except the Decatur..."

"Are you religious?" Clay interrupted. He did not want to hear any more of the story. The tone of the question, however, seemed directed as much at himself as at the detective.

"Religious?" the detective laughed. "Why the hell would you ask that?"

"You've probably seen some pretty terrible things as a police officer. I'm wondering if that makes it hard to believe in God?"

"You're right about seeing some ugly shit, but I don't give God much thought these days..."

"I would have expected," Clay said, talking over the top of the detective's words, "a person in your line of work would want a strong belief in God as a counterbalance against the violence."

"I said I didn't give God much thought. That's all. I didn't say anything about not believing."

"Okay. What I want to know, then, is has that belief changed because of the things you've experienced?"

The detective let the silence hang for an uncomfortable moment, his eyes fixed on Clay. "I'm not interested in talking about God with you, or anyone else, for that matter. What are you getting at?"

"The same thing you're trying to get at with your Indian war story. Aren't you looking to gauge my moral compass? Don't you want to know what I think of the settlers murdering the Indians? Isn't that the point of your story?"

"I doubt I'm capable of being that clever. But since you ask, were the settlers justified?"

Clay glanced down at the mess of papers spread across the floor and shook his head. The detective kept a casual air about him, but Clay knew better. He had come here for something very specific, and Clay was growing tired of waiting him out. "In those sorts of situations, it's good to be a God-fearing individual. Wouldn't you agree, Detective?"

"Are you going to answer my question?"

"You fought in Vietnam, didn't you?"

The detective's jaw tightened. "What does that have to do with anything?"

"Did you consider the killing of the Vietnamese people murder?" Clay asked. "Or was it justified because you did it in the name of God and Country? Did you ever wonder why you were in Southeast Asia to kill these people? Did you try to stop the killing? Did you demand those around you to stop? Did you do anything, Detective?"

"Boy," the detective said in a low growl, "you are treading on dangerous ground! You don't know what the fuck you're talking about, or what I went through over there! But let me be clear about one thing: if you ever ask, or say something that ignorant around me again, I will make certain you suffer because of it. Do you understand?"

Clay raised his hands in mock surrender. "I'm just trying to determine your sense of justice, Detective. That's all."

The detective took a long drink of beer in what appeared to be an effort to settle himself down. "You're not religious, I gather," he said, his voice still retaining a tight anger. "What do you believe in? Do you believe in anything? Morality? The law? Anything?"

The question made Clay smile. The detective wanted to get him to say something unscripted, maybe even incriminating. It was a good question, though. What did he believe in: God? Country? Blood? Family? History? Any of those would make a good answer. A good lie. "Sleep," he said. "I believe in the peaceful nothingness of sleep. How's that for a moral imperative?"

The detective, however, did not respond, just seemed to study Clay for a moment. "There was another thing I wanted to ask you about. You remember the woman's apartment we visited?"

Clay looked down at the brown bottle in his hand. He felt his throat tighten. This was what the detective had come for. "Sure. Did she turn up?"

"No, she hasn't turned up. I went back to her place, though, and found her personal diary. Some of the entries are quite interesting. She had this crazy idea that someone had murdered her grandmother. And get this, she thought it was related to the genealogy research her grandmother had been working on. Kind of like what you're doing here, I suppose. Anyway, in the diary, she mentions meeting up with a woman down in Pioneer Square. You're never going to guess what this woman's last name was."

Clay did not respond. He kept his eyes on the round opening of the beer bottle. Even though he had expected something like this, he still had to fight down a surge of panic, particularly since he had not known about the diary.

"She had the same last name as you."

"Odd," Clay said.

"What's your mom's name?"

"Eva."

The detective gave a tight laugh. "That's the name in the journal."

Clay took a drink of beer and turned his attention on the detective. "I don't know what to tell you. It's possible. My family owns a building down in Pioneer Square so my mom might have shown this woman around. You'd have to ask her about it."

The detective then mentioned something about another set of diary entries that described a man who, on several different occasions, had stood across the street from this woman's apartment building. The woman seemed to think he was there because of her, the detective said.

"Why the hell are you telling me this?" Clay asked, his mouth taking on a dry, sticky quality.

"That's the funny thing," the detective said, "the description of this guy sounds a little like you."

"You mean a skinny white guy?" he sneered. "Since only about half the city's population answers to that description, I guess she must be writing about me."

"She also describes a navy-blue sweatshirt similar to the one I've seen you wear."

"A navy-blue sweatshirt," Clay laughed. "You got me. No one else in this goddamn city could possibly match the description of a skinny white guy wearing a blue fucking hoody."

The detective smiled and took out a wad of papers and tossed it on the coffee table. "Those are copies of the most relevant diary entries. When you have a moment, look through those. I'd like to hear what you think."

Clay shook his head in disbelief. "Is this your indictment? You think I'm responsible for the disappearance of someone I've never met?"

"I'm just letting you know where I'm at with this." The detective paused as if considering what to say next. "You know your ignorant comment about Vietnam did remind me of something."

"I think you should go," Clay said. "I'm not interested in another one of your homilies."

"I'll make it short. Beside, you'll like this. After I got drafted, I spent six months in basic training before getting shipped off to Nam. You know how long that training lasted the first time I came under fire?"

"I really don't care."

"About three seconds. You can't practice how you're going to react when live rounds are whizzing by a few inches from your ear, or what it's like when pieces of skull from the guy next to you splatter across your uniform. I don't care how much training the government gives you. You aren't ready for the mess of that reality. I fared better than most. I had a bit of a knack for small details. I paid attention when something felt off. Shit, I could practically smell the enemy three clicks before an engagement. You know what I'm saying? During a patrol, if I got a feeling I should slow down and stop, I did. I didn't care who yelled at me to keep moving. And more times than not, either me or one of the other grunts found a booby trap nearby or an enemy ambush around the next turn in the trail. Other soldiers started to pay more attention to what I was doing than the platoon leader."

"Make your point, please."

The detective picked up the knight-crested ring. "Whose ring is this?"

"I already answered that question."

"How did it end up in this box of yours?"

Clay made a face as if he had bitten into something rotten. "I dug up my great-great-great grandfather and pulled the ring off his white, bony finger. Come on, we're going in circles here!"

"This is about trusting my instincts, just like I did in Vietnam," the detective explained. "And my instincts tell me to slow down with you. To pay attention."

"You know what's sad?" Clay said. "It sounds like you actually believe that. I keep waiting for you to start laughing and tell me you're joking. But you really think I have some connection with this woman. Hell, you probably think I have something to do with the murders in the Central District. You do know what circumstantial means, right? You are connecting dots that have nothing to do with each other. I have a generic ring that might match one she lost, and you interrogate me as if I'm a murder suspect. I don't have time for this. I'm about to lose my job, and you're questioning me about one of the dozens of random artifacts stashed in a box that up until a few days ago I didn't even know existed. And whatever you might think, I don't know anything about this woman. I've never met her, and I have no idea what happened to her!"

"Are you done?" the detective asked, his eyes locked on Clay in an unsuccessful attempt to intimidate him.

"I'm done. I also think it's time you left."

"In that stack of papers I threw on your table there," the detective said, "you'll also find some photocopied pages from a journal. Not sure what it means, but the woman repeatedly brings it up in her diary. It seems the journal covers a pioneer family's trip out West."

Clay tapped a fingernail against the side of the beer bottle. "Is that it?" he asked, sensing the detective still was not finished. "Or is your intuition telling you I was on the grassy knoll when JFK was killed?"

"No, that's about it. It could all be coincidences. I don't disagree with that. But when you start working on a case, all you have to go on at first is a lot of random-appearing events."

Clay picked up the loose copies of the pioneer journal. An almost unreadable flowing cursive covered each sheet, the same as the sheets he had picked off the top of the stack at the woman's apartment. He tried to focus on the looping letters and not the words themselves.

"I appreciate the beers," the detective said. "And I'll talk to the sergeant tomorrow and see what you can quote on the Central District and Portage Bay killings. Fair enough?"

Clay did not look up. Did not respond. A sense of relief settled over him as the apartment door opened and then slammed shut. It was at that point he became aware of the trembling in his hands. In his stomach. His legs. Not from anything the detective had said. It was something else. The lies. His own lies. How easy it was to talk without a single true word coming out of his mouth. The lies sounded so much better than the truth. If only he could make those words true and remove himself from reality.

209

Won't be a marker for Abby's grave. Just like Ma. Isn't right, though. Spent most of the day kneeling next to her grave and praying, letting her know how sorry I am. A woman from one of the other wagon trains helped me fashion a cross from the prairie grasses. I placed it on top of the fresh dug earth. Pa tends to the repair of the wagon. I stay away from him. He's nothing but anger and violence on account of losing most of the wagon's contents to the river...

Early Morning

The silence had changed. Clay, after lying down on the couch, pushed himself into a sitting position. The mix of alcohol and medication left him sluggish and groggy. It felt like he had lain down only a few minutes ago. The sound of rain seeped into the quiet. A car hydroplaned through a pool of water along the street. That wasn't where the silence had changed, though. There was something else. The chatter swirling through his head had shifted. It had become more like a whisper. Like walking into a room full of people telling secrets, the whispers so quiet as to be unintelligible.

Those quiet sounds of talking seemed so close and real. He looked around as if expecting to see something in the dark of the apartment. "Where are you?" he wondered out loud. A tickle of embarrassment filled him at the absurdly vacant sound of his voice. The rhythmless splash of water emptying out of a nearby gutter grew more pronounced.

Kiki's journal, a barely discernable outline on the coffee table, sat untouched, exactly where the detective had tossed the loose pieces of paper. Clay did not need to read any of it. Did not want to. Closing his eyes, he listened as the sounds of the rain take on the texture of color.

After some time, he reached over and switched on the table lamp next to the couch, his unsteady hand nearly knocking it over. He scanned the room: the mess of papers and documents remained untouched. He stood, went to the kitchen and turned on the light, and then to the bathroom and then the bedroom, turning on all the light fixtures until he had the entire apartment illuminated.

The clock on the stove showed 4:23 a.m. A crumpled-up piece of white construction paper, the type a child might use for a craft, sat on the kitchen counter. Clay picked it up and found an address written on it. He did not remember writing it, though, and did not understand why he would leave something like that out. It was a reckless move. Like leaving a bloody knife on the counter and daring the detective to come back and question him about it. Perhaps a part of him wanted the detective to come back and find it and figure out what it meant and where it led. Perhaps part of him wanted all of this to be over.

Morning

*T*o *believe in Jesus...* The radio voice faded slightly and a buzz of static filled in. *... this man wanted an argument, not wisdom...*

There used to be an AM station around the 1600 frequency that played local bands, but Clay had failed to find it and had given up looking, leaving it on the last station that had a signal. It was more about the sound than the content, the ambient noise wrestling with his disheveled thoughts.

Glancing at the map on the passenger seat, he slowed and took a right at the next intersection. The piece of construction paper sat next to the map. The address. Written out as if he were a child. As if he needed to be reminded. But Clay knew. As on the drive to Kiki's apartment a few days earlier, he knew what he was doing and where he was going. The map helped cultivate the lie, though, making it feel as if he needed help to find the house.

Adjusting the map, he found the tremor in his hand had worsened, like some sort of neurological disease. He returned his hand to the steering wheel. The physical exhaustion he felt contributed to the problem. But it was more than that. There was hate, too. Hate of himself. His history. Of her. The land. All of it. The taste of this hate filled his mouth like rotting flesh.

...tried to explain the idea of energy and how every unit of matter from living cells to inert stone is held together, created, by energy...

Clay took a left at the next street. He was close. A painful cramp twisted his gut, the kind of discomfort that made it feel like he might vomit.

...laughed and had to stop him. I told him what he was explaining was Divine Grace. The elegant nature of the universe comes from the divine will. I don't need scientific equations to explain ...

This was the street. The house number of the address ended in a six, so he focused on the right side of the street even though he knew where the house stood.

...the world is so much more than a predictable slave to instinctual ...

It took a couple of more blocks before he spotted the 1920s, yellow bungalow-style house. He slowed. It all appeared so familiar. Yet unreal. Like an image from a dream, or a half-forgotten memory. The yard was overgrown. A red and white "For Rent" sign stood barely visible within the tall weeds. From the backyard, a giant cedar tree towered above the roof. Part of him wanted to keep driving, to pretend that seeing the house was enough. But those sorts of lies only worked if he could disregard the reality of the situation; and that no longer seemed possible. Clay parked to the north of the property. The car continued to run; AM static buzzed like a hive of bees. He hesitated to turn the car off, wondering if there was still time to turn around and leave. With a counterclockwise twist of the ignition, the radio static ceased, and the engine shuddered to a stop. In the silence, his head filled with the sound of whispering voices, each one urging him in a different direction.

Stepping out of the car and into the mild morning air, he did a quick study of the area as he approached the house. No cars. The sidewalk in both directions was empty. She grew up here, he thought. He tilted his head back. Gray clouds. Subtle wisps of wind.

A cracked and uneven walkway led to the front door. At the small, concrete porch, he cupped his hands against a dirt-caked picture window and saw an empty living room. No furniture. Only the dusty hardwood floors and an old broom that leaned against a river-rock fireplace.

He stepped off the raised concrete slab and walked to the back of the house. The backyard was just as overgrown as the front with nearly the entire space filled with a dense mix of un-pruned shrubs and three-foot-tall weeds.

At the base of the large cedar tree, someone had nailed irregularly sized pieces of 2x4s into the trunk to form a crude ladder. The weeds around the tree were trampled, evidence of Clay's recent activity there. Looking up, he saw that the ladder led to a plywood-constructed treehouse built over several of the tree's large lower branches.

As he stood there, the world grew very quiet and still, as if something were in the process of passing away.

Clay took ahold of one of the rectangular rungs and started to climb. Upon reaching the top, he eased himself onto a piece of aged plywood. In the silent, unmoving air, he could hear his own breathing. The thick tangle of overhead branches allowed very little light to penetrate the space. Even so, he could still see the series of letters carved into the side of the tree. With his index finger, he traced the lines of each letter: K I K I S O B L U. Kiki's full name. A Duwamish princess. He wondered how old she had been when she carved the letters into the tree. Nine? Ten? The surface of the letters felt smooth, as if the wind and the rain had produced them over a long period of time. How often had her grandmother used her full name? Had she used it when she was upset at her granddaughter? Had she whispered her granddaughter's full name and followed that with an embrace? Taking a prescription bottle from his pocket, he shook out two pills, put them in his mouth, and used a nearby water bottle to wash them down. He would sleep now and wait until dark to begin the long trip east.

Before lying down, he checked on the unmoving figure next to him. The zip ties binding her ankles and wrists, along with the gag, remained firmly in place. The ratchet straps continued to hold her down. She breathed. She was alive. He vaguely recalled giving her water and a bit of food at some point in the last day or two. These recollections felt like someone else's memories, though, or like something that had happened a long time in the past.

He reached over and put a hand close to her face, careful to avoid touching her. Her body radiated an unnatural heat, like a fever; an incontinent odor hung in the air, mixing with the scent of the cedar tree sap. He was not sure how he felt about all of this. Was this the point? To expand and prolong the suffering despite the wrongness of it? And it did feel wrong. He knew that. Felt the nausea of it tearing at his gut. And so he tried to push these unwelcome thoughts aside, ignore them, block them out as one more piece of an intolerable orchestra of noise striving to unhinge his mental stability.

A thrumming filled his head as he lay down. He watched her and waited for sleep to take hold of him. He saw a bit of himself there, like a reflection; the fear and pain etched into her face; the absence of peace; something, perhaps, about the shape of the nose or cheeks.

It was better this way, he thought, closing his eyes and trying to ignore his own thoughts. He listened, attempting to pick out the subtle fluctuations, the different textures of sounds around him as if it were music, or a language he needed to translate.

The Road

The road stretched for miles in a north-south direction. The two lanes traveled across an undulating landscape of hillocks to converge into a single black point in the far distance.

The car idled next to a gas pump. The gas tank was near empty. It was difficult to tell how long he had been sitting there. He switched the car off. His head hurt as with a bad hangover. Not enough sleep. Too much medication.

He had no idea where he had stopped. The terrain had a gentle, almost imperceptible roll to it, all of it surrounded by endless swathes of amber-colored wheat. He must be somewhere in the Palouse, he guessed. Eastern Washington. Or maybe he had crossed over into Idaho. The landscape offered no clues.

He rubbed his face with the back of his hands. His entire body hurt. He looked over at the small café that sat a dozen yards from the gas pumps. Perhaps if he ate. The café's weathered faux-log exterior had seen better days. A small metal sign near the door identified the restaurant as The Oasis. Gravel made up the space around the café and gas pumps. He was not sure about the time of day. It felt early. The low-angled light added to that feeling. Patches of blue were visible amongst the cirrus clouds streaking across the upper atmosphere. Did that make it Thursday? Friday?

A gust of wind sent a spray of dust swirling around the car.

Clay clenched the steering wheel and rested his head against his whitened knuckles as a cold, dry air worked its way into the car. He listened for any sounds, any kind of movement coming from the back of the vehicle. Nothing. Only the wind. His slow breathing. The eddying of his tormented thoughts.

It was not until the woman from the restaurant came out and tapped on the driver-side window that he brought his head back up. The woman had her hands cupped against the side of the dirty glass and was staring at him.

Clay rolled down the window.

"You all right in there?" She looked to be in her early forties. She had her sandy-blond hair wrapped in a loose bun.

"I'm fine," Clay said.

"Do you need gas?"

"Yes."

"Honey, why don't you go inside the restaurant and rest a little?" she said. "My name is Anne. You go ahead and go inside. The biscuits and gravy are the specialty here." The woman went around to the other side to start pumping the gas as wisps of dust swirled into the car.

It was okay, he thought. It was going to be okay. As he stepped out of the car, his back and leg muscles were stiff.

The heater above the café's front door blew a rush of warm air across the surface of his skin, a welcome relief from the cold cemented into his bones. There were no other customers. He sat in a booth next to the window. A red-and-white-checkered cloth covered the table. He picked up a menu wedged between the napkin holder and the plastic ketchup and mustard dispensers. The words on the menu blurred and then focused. He could not remember the last time he had eaten.

Maybe it was the warm air of the restaurant, or perhaps the release from the stress of driving, but he put his arms on the table and rested his head on top of them even as he warned himself to stay awake for fear he might talk in his sleep or walk outside and show someone the contents of the trunk.

A bell rang somewhere. Clay forced himself to sit up, wiping a bit of spittle from his mouth. He took a quick look around to remember where he was. Someone must have come into the café and caused the little bell above the door to ring. There were several other people in the restaurant now. Out the window, he saw his car parked in front of the building. Had he moved it? The sun appeared higher in the sky. A dust devil swirled near the gas pumps, small pieces of gravel pinging against the metal surface.

He looked down at the menu opened in front of him.

A few moments later, Anne approached the table. "You ready to order?"

He saw the words printed on the menu but could not read any of them. "Maybe a little more time, please."

"No problem," she said. "Like I mentioned before, the cook does a nice job with the biscuits and gravy."

The woman disappeared behind the lunch counter and into the kitchen area beyond. The plaintive voice of Patsy Cline played from somewhere in the back. Clay stared at the menu. The twang of guitar crackled behind Cline's soft voice as she sang of a broken heart.

When the woman returned, Clay, still unable to read anything from the menu, ordered the biscuits and gravy.

After several moments of indecision, he stood up from the table. He needed to call Detective Carpenter. His stiff and tired body ached as he made his way to the payphone next to the men's bathroom at the back of the restaurant. He inserted a dollar in quarters and dialed the number.

"Clay! How are you, my friend? Better yet, where are you?"

"I'm at home," he answered. The lie had become his first reaction, even if it did not make a difference whether he told the truth or not.

"Perfect. I'm coming over."

"Before you do that, I have a question."

"All right. I have a few questions for you as well."

"Have you found Kiki?"

There was a momentary pause on the other end. "Funny you should ask. Where did you say you were?" The detective's voice sounded far away.

"Home." A movement drew Clay's eyes out the café's window as a semi-truck rumbled down the highway.

"Did you find her?" he repeated.

"You know we haven't found her, Clay. That's what I want to talk to you about. Do you know where she is?"

"No."

"Give yourself a moment to think about that. I think you do know where she is."

Clay leaned against the phone, putting his weight against his arm to keep it from shaking. "Is that your intuition talking again?"

"No. I spoke to your mother."

"What does that have to do with anything?"

"She told me about her encounter with Kiki down at the Pioneer Square building. She seems to think Kiki and your family have some kind of connection."

"My family has lived in Seattle a long time. We have connections with all sorts of people."

"I also looked through the boxes you left at your mother's place. There were things in there from Kiki's apartment. Why were there things from her apartment in those boxes, Clay?" the detective asked.

Clay closed his eyes. In that moment, he considered hanging up the phone. He vaguely recalled taking a couple of boxes to Eva's, but he could not remember why

221

he had done that. He should have known the detective would talk to her. Perhaps he had dropped the boxes off for that very reason, hoping the detective would find them; it was difficult to know for certain with his thoughts so scattered.

This information was enough, though. He had wanted to know if the detective had found anything; and he had. He could hang up now.

"Why did you go back to her apartment?"

"I never went back."

"Where are you, Clay?"

"I'll come see you in a couple of days," he said. "We can talk more then."

"Is she still alive?"

Clay focused on the music playing in the kitchen. It had changed. "Ring of Fire." Johnny Cash.

"Is she with you?" the detective asked.

Clay did not answer.

"It's not too late, Clay. You still have time to do the right thing. You understand? Why don't you come in? We'll talk about it. I can help you. But you need come in. If you don't, I'll get a warrant…"

The threat drew Clay back into the conversation. "A warrant!" he said with a clipped laugh. The exhaustion, the built-up stress, all of it made an argument with the detective an almost welcomed release. "What makes you think you have grounds for a warrant? Some papers in a box at my mom's place. A suspicion that I went to the woman's apartment. Are judges issuing warrants based on an officer's intuition now? Is that the legal bar we're working with?" he asked, his voice rising. "To be honest, I wish we could sit down and talk. I would do that if I thought it would help. But at this point, there isn't much that can be done. Not anymore. Not unless you can go back and change history. Can you do that for me, Detective? I know how much you love history. Can you go back and change it?"

"One way or another, I'm going to get you to come in. It's better…"

There was more Clay wanted to say, explanations he wanted to give on history and cultural legacies the detective did not appear to understand. But it was time to go. Past time. Clay carefully placed the phone back in its shiny metal cradle; a shudder quivered through his body. The detective knew what he was doing. That was all he wanted to confirm.

Returning to the table, he managed a few bites of the biscuits and chunky gravy before his stomach cramped and made it impossible to eat any more. Clay stood, took his wallet from his front pocket, and tossed an uncertain amount of cash on the table for the gas and meal. It was going to be okay, he thought. But he couldn't seem to leave the table, continuing to stare down at the nearly full plate of food.

"You want me to box that up?" Anne asked, coming up from behind him.

"No." Clay avoided looking at her, afraid of what she might see in his face. He turned and walked out the front door.

Back in the car, he picked through the handful of prescription bottles scattered on the passenger seat. He started the car. The benzodiazepine bottle was the first one he opened up. The next bottle was zolpidem. He took one pill from each and swallowed them without water. He wanted sleep. A deep, forgetful state of unconsciousness.

He put the car in gear and got back on the road heading south. The land seemed so much the same in every direction. Only a few scattered trees. Cold. So much space.

The car hit a dip in the road, lifting Kiki's body off the floor of the trunk; the return impact sent a fresh shock of pain through her battered left shoulder and hip. The added physical suffering prompted a barely audible grunt. Slivers of gray light filtered into the dark space from cracks in the car's frame; the trunk's thin, rough carpet offered little protection against the hard metal undercarriage as the vibration of the engine rattled the floor. The smell of oil and dirt, metal and exhaust burned the soft tissue on the inside of her nose; the taste of blood and bile tinged her mouth.

It hurt to breathe. A gag cut across the dried and cracked skin of her lips and cheeks. Zip ties secured her hands and feet behind her back and prevented her from bracing against the constant jolt of the car's movements. She no longer felt the cold, but her body shook anyway; and the once grinding hunger had slipped to the background as an almost forgotten ache.

As she struggled against the restraints, the ties dug deeper into the open sores cutting across her wrists and ankles. She let out a muffled scream. Again. Pain seared through her dry throat. She cried. Again. Her body unable to produce tears.

In time, she slipped into a fevered dream about her grandmother. The sound of her grandmother's warm and quiet laughter filled the hollow, metal space like music. Beautiful. Reassuring. Her grandmother's hand stroked Kiki's hair and her voice calmed and comforted her, reminding her that everything would be okay; the two of them would be together soon, and Kiki would be safe again.

Sunrise

Afrigid, low-angled light filtered into the car. Clay shivered and pulled his jacket tighter. His movements were slow, lethargic. Beyond the ice-frosted windows, the sky appeared a clear, crystal blue. Transparent and cold. He pushed himself up, slid the key into the ignition, and started the car to get the heater going. He zipped up his jacket and then rolled down the window to circulate some fresh air into the stale atmosphere that stank of day-old hamburger and greasy French fries.

Tall grass surrounded the car. He was parked along a gravel road. The Snake River meandered west a couple of hundred yards away. The muscles of his arms and lower back felt cramped and tired. Blisters peppered his palms, and dirt covered his pants and jacket.

The sun seemed to hold still as the car warmed up enough to send hot air through the heater vents. It took time to remember where he was, to remind himself he still had work to complete. She was out there now. Waiting. Minutes passed before he turned the car off and opened the door. The orange disk of the sun hung low in the east. No wind. The crisp, sweet smell of the river filled the cold air as if spring and a rebirth were only days away.

He walked into the dew-speckled grass and followed a freshly trodden path that paralleled the river where three oval shaped islands dotted a wide-open expanse of water, each grassy island like a giant steppingstone.

According to the diary, the family had crossed this same open stretch of river on the passage West. Abby had drowned here. Maybe that was what made this place feel so familiar.

The grass brushed against the backs of his hands. The unceasing chatter of the river grew louder as he walked along the sloping hill. In the near distance, the handle of a shovel stood above the waist-high wheatgrass. Blood from the sores on his hands stained the top end of the shovel's wooden shaft. Mounds of dirt encircled the surrounding ground. Reaching the spot, he turned his eyes in the direction of the sky, towards the empty, opalescent sky, away from the loamy smell of earth and decay. If he could fly, he would travel far away from this place. This history. This world.

Below him sat a well-proportioned rectangular pit. The hollow was about five feet deep, seven feet long, and six feet wide. A half-exhumed human skull and ribcage rested at the bottom. To the right of the bones lay Kiki's motionless body. She was on her side facing away from the skeleton; bound together, her legs and arms twisted behind her, creating a bow-like arc to her torso. Beyond the tangle of black hair, a strip of red cloth stretched across her mouth and around her head.

Clay felt himself slip back and land against a hump of dirt. The bones of his great-great-great-aunt still overlooked the river where she had drowned.

Clay watched the shallow rise and fall of Kiki's chest. He could not remember the last time she had eaten or had water.

Kiki's leg made a reflexive twitch. He took the shovel and dropped a bit of dirt near her feet. Was this it? Was he going to bury her here? He dug the shovel into the dirt and sprinkled it further up Kiki's legs. Nothing. Movement had ceased.

How would he hide after this? Did he even want to hide?

It was not until the dirt hit her head that there was another small convulsion. She must be exhausted, he thought. Perhaps sleeping. He struggled to move, to pick up more dirt and drop it on her. He stood there. This was it. He stuck the shovel back into the dirt. It was done. The lie. A dream. Clay knelt and let himself slip into the grave. The noises in his head grew louder. Like drowning. The louder it became, the less he heard until the sounds filled his entire body. He made space for himself between the bones and Kiki. He lay down. Each thought and movement weighed on him. Like an unbearable pressure. Each thought scrambled to make sense of itself. Self-referencing. Self-consoling.

"We'll wait together," he whispered to Kiki. But she didn't move. There was no more movement. No breathing. Nothing. Only stillness. The smell of earth. An iridescent blue sky above.